Assignment Abacus

By L. P. Davies

Assignment Abacus

L. P. DAVIES

PUBLISHED FOR THE CRIME CLUB BY

DOUBLEDAY & COMPANY, INC.

GARDEN CITY, NEW YORK

1975

All of the characters in this book
are fictitious, and any resemblance
to actual persons, living or dead,
is purely coincidental.

Library of Congress Cataloging in Publication Data
Davies, Leslie Purnell
Assignment abacus
I. Title.
PZ4.D2565As   [PR6054.A886]   823'.9'14
ISBN 0-385-01799-5
Library of Congress Catalog Card Number 74-33635

Assignment Abacus

⚅ ONE ⚅

The helicopter, glistening silver and blue, rode the cloudless early evening sky. Its pilot, thirtyish, bareheaded, wearing a shabby leather jacket with a once-white fur collar, leaned forward in his bucket seat the better to assess the view ahead. Far to the right was a thin thread of silver.

"Water," he identified, and tracked it down on the folded map attached to one side of the instrument panel, announcing with some satisfaction: "That's it. Blackwater Reservoir." And when his solitary passenger didn't react: "This is it, Mr. Maskell."

Boyd Maskell, silent throughout the long journey, looked up from the sheaf of papers on his lap. "What's that?"

The pilot smiled faintly. "Journey's end. More or less. Only a matter now of locating the landing area. Village, first. What's it called?" He consulted the slip of paper attached to the section of map. "Kirkmalcolm. About thirty miles south of Blackwater Reservoir, it says. That's the reservoir over there. Loch Leven on the left." He leaned sideways to peer downward. "I reckon we've overshot." He took the helicopter round in a juddering tight half-circle, the mottled September purple and brown landscape swinging up to fill the window on Maskell's right, falling away to leave blue-green emptiness as they levelled out.

The pilot, leaning forward again, whistled softly through nicotine-stained teeth, breaking off to offer: "Rannock Moor, it says, that little lot down there. Doesn't look too cheery from up here." He seemed anxious to make up for the silence of the last four hours. "You know this part of the world, Mr. Maskell?"

Maskell, collecting his papers together, shook his head without looking up. "This is my first time in Scotland."

"Haggis and pibrochs. All right if you go for that sort of thing." The pilot throttled back. "That looks like it down on the left." Grey and blue oblongs clustered cosily about the lighter grey ribbons of a small complication of roads. "Not much of a place. Now, where is it we set down?" He read off from the paper: " 'House about one mile north of village, suitable landing site at rear.' One thing, no worry there, you can set these babies down on a kitchen table."

Maskell snapped one briefcase shut and bent, silken dark-brown hair falling over his narrow forehead, to set it alongside the unopened, locked case which contained the more important papers.

"I take it this is your first time out here," he observed, more for something to say than anything else.

"There it is." The pilot swung the machine round again. "I'll know the way next time. That's if there is a next time. Only been on the job a few days. This is my first assignment. Trial period." He grinned as he manoeuvred the 'copter down. "To see how I make out. Like I'd never done any chopper work before." He shrugged, no rancour in his voice. "So what the hell. Takes all sorts. Friend of yours, maybe." He glanced briefly sideways. "Long streak of a bloke; spoke like he'd got something stuck in his mouth; square face that looked like it hadn't seen the light of day in years; Lord Muck on the top floor of the highest high-rise on the South Bank. I forget his name—"

A sketchy and exaggerated description, but nonetheless evocative. Maskell stared at the cratered brown profile. "Not Agnew—Pearson Agnew?"

"I don't know about the Pearson bit, but Agnew's right enough." Now the machine was hovering, dipping like a stately rocking horse, the steady thrum-thrum of the blades became muted. The pilot spared time for another sideways glance. "You sound surprised."

Frowning, Maskell leaned back in his seat. In the financial conglomeration that was Saturn the chain of command was pretty much the same as in an army. And generals don't deal directly with lorry drivers. Unless there is some very special reason.

The helicopter touched down with a barely perceptible jolt. The engine sound died, the thrumming slowed and stopped. The silence was intense.

"That's it, Mr. Maskell," the pilot said with a certain air of formality. "Hope you enjoyed the trip." He leaned across to open the door on Maskell's side, adding with small irony: "Hope you enjoy your stay here. Holiday, is it, then?"

Maskell ignored both the invitation to leave the machine, and the question.

"How did you come to get this job?" he asked.

"Choppering in general, or ferrying you out here?"

"With Saturn."

"Who-er? Never heard of it."

"You're working for them," Maskell said shortly. "This is one of their machines."

"I wondered about that planet insignia on the tail. Well, Biddulph Electronics are the boyos doing the paying. Got word about the job from a drinking friend, went along to the address he gave and a starchy bint in the ground office shunted me directly up to his nibs in the penthouse."

So, not a member of Earlam's private flying corps, but personally engaged by Agnew, and not through the regular channels. And, if Maskell had read the signs correctly, being paid by Agnew—for Biddulph Electronics was his own personal company—and taken on specifically for this assignment. This single trip now, or to cover the whole thing?

"You say you don't know if you'll be making this same trip again?" he queried.

"I don't even know where I'm to report back to now," the pilot told him, and looked pointedly at the dashboard clock. Ten minutes past five. "All I know is I'm to drop you off here, refuel at"—he consulted his typed instructions again—"Dumbarton, and receive further instructions there." He leaned sideways to look past Maskell's shoulder in the direction of the house, frowning. "We must have made a racket coming in. Where is everybody? Ah—" His face cleared. "Your welcoming committee."

Maskell sought the reason for the familiar sound of a name. And found it. Agnew—Agnew again—owned a house on the outskirts of Dumbarton, one of his country retreats.

"If you'd like to get out," the pilot offered with mild impatience, "I'll hand your gear down to you."

Maskell climbed stiffly out into the cool evening. There was a pleasant fresh scent to the air. On three sides the world was patchworked green and purple and brown, stretching in gentle waves to a horizon of floating violet mountains. They had landed on a patch of rough grass that had perhaps once been a trimmed lawn at the rear of a not particularly large or attractive house. Not the sort of surroundings the earl usually selected for his directors' meetings. But then, the extraordinary nature of the coming meeting, the question of security, obviously called for something out of the ordinary.

The only trees in this lonely Scottish world grew close about the flat-roofed, two-storeyed house with flaking faded yellow walls and small-paned Georgian windows, most of them uncurtained. Two sets of narrow french windows gave on to the crumbling surface of what must once have been a fairly imposing terrace. One set of windows was open. Through them must have come the thin, grey-haired man who walked unhurriedly towards them.

"Here we are, sir," the pilot said, bending out of the plane to nudge Maskell's shoulder with one of the briefcases. Maskell took it quickly from him, the locked case of private papers that normally he never let out of his grasp when travelling.

"May I take that for you, sir?" An unctuous, obsequious voice. Maskell turned to its grey-haired, discreetly dressed owner. "I'll carry this one myself. There's another, and two suitcases."

"Very good, sir." But the grey-haired man hesitated. "You *are* Mr. Boyd Maskell, sir?"

Maskell, well-accustomed to the situation, felt no resentment at the implication that in appearance he bore not the slightest resemblance to the popular conception of the new breed of alert, incisive and ruthless young executives, the go-ahead whizz-kids of commerce, that his loose, silken dark-brown hair, narrow, almost womanly features, large, shadowed eyes and smooth olive skin took all of ten from his thirty-two years to leave the impression of a gauche, overgrown schoolboy. That he wore the approved business uniform of well-cut dark-blue suit, striped shirt, semi-stiff white collar and broad patterned tie helped in no way at all.

"I'm Maskell," he said dryly. "And you are—?"

"Howard, sir. Welcome to Malven." The grey-haired man tucked the other briefcase under his arm and reached for the two suitcases that covered the ten days Maskell had had his man pack for, not knowing how long the meeting was going to last, how long he might have to stay on afterwards out here in the wilds. The breeze seemed suddenly to have intensified, to have become cold and raw. A bird called far away, the thin shriek of sound lonely and eerie.

"All the best, then, Mr. Maskell," the pilot offered with a hint of sarcasm, and was all set to shut himself back in the comparative comfort of his machine.

"Will you please wait," Howard said to him. "I have orders for you. If you will wait, I will bring them out to you."

The other shrugged resignedly. "You're the gaffer." He leaned back in his seat, stretching luxuriously, arms clasped behind the shabby fur collar.

"Am I the first to arrive?" Maskell enquired, following the laden Howard across the coarse grass, up three crumbling steps and across the cracked concrete of the terrace.

"You are, sir." A soft, very precise, and for some reason, irritating voice.

"Have you been out here long?"

"Only a few days, sir." Howard stepped politely aside for Maskell to precede him through the french windows. "You will find the layout of the place somewhat confusing at first, sir. One gathers that the original building was much smaller, and that through the years additions have been built on with little regard for the—ah—finished product."

Irritating, both way of speaking and nasal intonation, Maskell thought again. And it was so, he decided, because there was the impression of someone playing the part of the perfect family retainer and overdoing that role.

He followed across the large, sparely furnished room, and was invited by gesture to lead the way through a facing door into a second room, similar in shape and size, but this furnished far less austerely, with a centrepiece grouping of dark leather settee and armchairs. The matching pair of cannon on the mantelpiece and the framed period military prints on the anonymous brown wall-paper helped give the room its male atmosphere. No books in evidence, so a lounge rather than a library.

The wall facing the door was broken by three high, narrow small-paned windows that overlooked the front of the house. Not a particularly inviting view: another strip of crumbling terrace—Maskell wondered how long the place had stood empty before Saturn's Property Group had bought it—a drive, more moss than gravel, a line of stunted bushes and then the ever-lasting expanse of lonely moor with its eternal background frieze of violet mountains. But not quite so empty a landscape as that at the rear of the house, for here the drive passed between stone pillars to join a road of sorts; and that road wound its way to-wards the distant low roofs and square church tower of the village—what had the pilot called it?—Kirkmalcolm.

Howard's discreet, over-well-mannered cough was attention-attracting rather than throat-clearing. He had set down one of the cases in order to open a door in the righthand wall. Now he waited for Maskell to precede him through it.

Into the hall—entrance, not dining, but large enough, with its high raftered ceiling, to be the latter. A broad staircase, solidly utilitarian, completely undecorative, led up to a narrow gallery.

Howard deposited the cases on the bare stone-flagged floor, and was deferentially apologetic.

"If you wouldn't mind waiting a moment, sir, while I deliver his orders to the pilot." Apparently in the envelope he picked up from the three-legged bamboo table in the corner by the front door. "Then I will show you to your room."

Maskell set his briefcase down at his feet and turned to watch the other go. Orders in a sealed envelope, for God's sake, as if this were some military operation. He permitted himself a small sideways smile. So secrecy was essential, that was plain common sense, but this seemed to be carrying the cloak-and-dagger stuff a bit too far. Agnew's theatrical touch, he assumed; everything pointed to his being the organising genius behind at least this stage of the operation. He must have had his reasons; Pearson Agnew always had good reasons for everything he did.

Maskell shivered, becoming aware of the coldness of the place, of a kind of damp chill rising from the worn flags. It had been comfortably warm in the helicopter, the pilot's fur-collared jacket obviously mainly for show, another unofficial uniform of the species, and so he had felt no need for a coat. He hoped that Judd, his usually farsighted manservant, had anticipated a final destination where September might be colder than in London, and had packed accordingly.

Howard seemed a long time away. Perhaps chatting with the pilot, although he hadn't given the impression of being a chatty type. And then it suddenly occurred to Maskell to wonder why, when the seemingly efficient Howard heard the helicopter approaching, as he certainly must have done, he hadn't brought the envelope out with him when he came to meet its passenger, instead of having to put himself to the trouble of a second trip out to the machine.

While Maskell wondered at the apparent oversight, a distant throbbing was the now familiar sound of the rotor starting up again. Picking up his briefcase he walked back through the two rooms to stand in the still open french windows to watch the machine, already airborne, canting steeply as it swung round, the low evening sun tinting the fuselage silver with rose, blazing blindingly back where it was reflected from the bulbous glass enclosing the pilot and the now empty passenger seat. Or what *should* have been the empty passenger seat.

It was only when Maskell saw that the seat was occupied, that there were two people in the machine, one with grey hair, that the realisation came that he hadn't passed Howard in the house, and that the stretch of wind-flattened grass where the helicopter sleds had rested was empty.

TWO

The helicopter, canting steeply, ablaze with the evening sun, swept over the house and away out of sight, the sound of its engine gradually dying away.

Frowning, puzzled—no more—at what had happened, Maskell closed the windows one-handed and walked back to the hall where his luggage stood in a lonely pile in the middle of the expanse of bare grey stone.

Feeling somewhat foolish he raised his voice, calling: "Hullo? Is anyone there?" From halfway up the broad dark-wood staircase he shouted again. The house sounded empty, felt empty.

He returned to the hall, still carrying the briefcase, to start off on a small tour of inspection, first opening the door that faced the front door. A large, airy room for the kitchen it obviously was. A yellow-stone sink, old as the hills, stood under the window that framed a view that was already becoming monotonous to one accustomed to city scenes. An ugly and enormous black iron range—did people still use such monstrosities?—occupied the whole of the lefthand wall. A set of flimsy-looking cupboards filled the other; the red-tiled floor was bare.

Ten minutes later, quarter to six now by the grandfather clock in the opposite corner to the bamboo table in the hall, and he had confirmed what he had already been certain of, that he was now alone in the house. Of the remaining four rooms on the ground floor, two were unfurnished, the other two only sketchily fitted out with unmatching bits and pieces. Upstairs he had found five of the bedrooms, the five larger, to be empty, giving the impression, by an accumulation of dust and small debris, of having been that way for years. There were two bathrooms, one seemingly only recently modernised, and two smaller bedrooms equipped with single beds and wardrobes and a few other of the bare necessities, one showing signs of recent occupancy, presumably where Howard had slept.

Becoming aware that he was still holding the briefcase, Maskell set it down alongside the other things in the hall, and spent a few minutes taking stock of the situation. The only explanation for this present state of affairs that made any kind of sense was that Agnew intended staffing the place with his own people, not trusting the care of the party, when it was assembled for Wednesday's meeting, to people he didn't know. Howard, like the pilot, must have been engaged on a temporary basis only, there to start the task of bringing an apparently long-dead house back to life, his last chore being to greet the first arrival.

If that, or something like it, was the explanation for this deserted, partly furnished house, then it was reasonable to assume that the personnel nominated by Agnew to staff the place must right now be somewhere nearby—almost certainly bedded down in the village—their signal to move in being the helicopter's departure. And when they did move in, there was a hell of a lot for them to do before Wednesday. Today was Monday. That left only one day, just twenty-four hours, for them to finish furnishing the place and rendering it suitably habitable for a bunch of top-level executives used to an existence of Rolls Royces and penthouse luxury suites in West End hotels.

Hands on blue-clad hips, Maskell gazed round the dreary hall, remembering the condition of the rest of the house, in particular the empty bedrooms, picturing the fridgeless, ill-equipped kitchen, the Victorian horrors of yellow-stone sink and iron cooking range. It was simply impossible. No matter how many people Agnew had engaged, no matter if they were waiting round the corner with all the necessary furniture, fittings and kitchen utensils, it would take at least a week—no, the workmen of today being what they are, more than a week—to turn this bleak and filthy mausoleum into anything even approaching a suitable venue for such a meeting.

So what was it all about? What the devil was going on? He was certain in his own mind that Agnew was in charge of operations. It was out of the question to even consider the possibility of his having made an error in the timing or the place chosen. Agnew didn't make errors. Maskell nibbled pensively on his lower lip. The helicopter had picked him up at the designated place: a small airfield on the outskirts of Coventry that the earl always used when in the Midlands. Judging by what had happened, Howard must have known when he came out to the plane that he would be leaving by it. And yet he had seen fit to go off without saying a word. No explanation, nothing. Unusual, to say the least. It was a pretty safe bet, Maskell felt, to assume he had been obeying orders, sealed or otherwise. And that was all. On the face of it, the whole operation had gone off smoothly, with no trace of confusion, no hint of any kind of hitch. And before take-off in Coventry?

A week ago today; that was when it had started. Ten o'clock and Monday morning in the earl's private office in his Mayfair penthouse suite. The usual bright morning bustle of junior exec-utives—sleek, up-and-coming young men with carefully cul-tivated alert expressions—and deceptively languid, discreetly per-fumed secretaries, all tall and sleek, all cast from the same mould, only the colouring different. Agnew was there, of course, and Brownlea and Henderson, senior directors, grey-haired both. And Sir John was there; leaving as Maskell arrived. But nothing unusual about that. For all his leonine, solid-as-a-rock appear-ance, Conrad Earlam—sometimes called "the earl"—was a sick man. At seventy-five, with three heart attacks under his belt, all of them fortunately minor, he had his own private physician, and that physician visited him every day. And when you are the man who sits on top of the peak of the mountain that is the Saturn Cartel, possibly the richest, certainly the most commercially influential man in London, perhaps Europe, then you can afford the best. And the best is Sir John Mellish-Rae, late of seven universities, late of four London hospitals, late of Harley Street and onetime consultant to the royal family.

Maskell stared unseeingly at the hideous blue and green stained-glass panels of the front door.

It was possible, and this was a thought that had already oc-curred to him, that news of the discovery of the treacherous share manipulation had caused the earl to have another small attack. Certainly, old and tired as he was, it must have upset him pretty badly, although, thinking back, Agnew and the others hadn't seemed too concerned. But Sir John's visit, normally a routine five-minute affair, had lasted for almost an hour. He was leaving just as Maskell, summoned by telephone, arrived, his raised hand and brief nod the gestures of royalty acknowledging respect and adulation.

One of the senior directors, old Brownlea it had been, had asked Maskell to wait in one of the side offices usually reserved for the more important visitors. He had been kept waiting for over half an hour, and that was something unusual indeed in a world where life was organised down to each and every last minute.

And at last Agnew had come, calm and unruffled. "Ah, Maskell. So sorry to have kept you hanging about." In his early forties, no more, and so the youngest of the senior directors. Ageless in a wax-white way, with oversquare face, thick lips, sleek, brushed-back black hair and hollowed eyes. "Coffee; shall I send for coffee?"

"They brought me some a while back," Maskell said, as always finding it difficult to keep the quite unwarranted dislike of the older man from showing in his face and voice.

And then to the reason for his having been unexpectedly called from an important outside accounting check to head office.

Saturn either owned or had interests of one kind or another in something over four hundred different companies, ranging in size from those giants whose names were household words, whose plants covered thousands of acres, down to the small but highly specialised concerns that were often little more than one-man back-street affairs. Its lifeblood was money. It existed off the ebb and flow of the financial tide as it eddied about the rocks of the Exchange, Wall Street, the Bourse and a gathering of six quiet men in Zurich who were known simply and collectively as Le Bloque. It provided jobs for its five thousand employees and profit for its board by knowing the exact moment when to sell or buy. And to help it know when that moment was, it employed the finest brains in the country.

Maskell had come into Saturn by chance and not by choice. Born in St. John's Wood, his father a solicitor, he had passed through the usual strata of more expensive education. He had left Oxford at nineteen with a not over-remarkable degree in chemistry, to join Bayard's, a small chemical manufacturing firm. Two years later Bayard's had been taken over by Saturn, then only a ghost of its present self. He had spent the next eleven years behind office desks instead of stained benches, each a little larger than the one before. As Saturn had grown, so it had taken him up with it. Now he was one of the ten junior directors and head of that branch of the cartel called Forward Projection and Clear Intention, its main functions the evaluation of the present state of companies, an assessment of their potential future and the resultant tendering of advice to the market section as to how they should react to that assessment.

Inevitably, in a section of that kind, secrecy was of prime importance. Any leak of Saturn's information and intentions would have an immediate effect on the Exchange. Fortunes could be made, and lost, within hours. A slip of the tongue could take millions from the value of a company, add millions to another, might conceivably bring Saturn toppling.

It was to prevent any such leak, unintentional or otherwise, that the Bluesheets had come into being. They were part of a security measure that so far had been completely effective. At the end of every third month an assessment of holdings was compiled, a kind of stocktaking, with every asset held by the cartel listed and valued, so that on four days out of every year Conrad Earlam knew exactly how much he was worth, knew whether his fortune had risen or fallen in the past three months. But only he and his board of directors ever saw that final figure. Until it came into his hands the vital figures representing Saturn's holdings in each of its four hundred companies, printed on flimsy blue paper, were in code—a code too complicated to be memorised, too complex to be broken down. Even in the unlikely event of a complete set of four hundred and more coded returns falling into the wrong hands, it would be impossible for the owner of those hands, using any system of trial and error, to work out the code, even if he had a computer at his disposal. There was only one copy of the code in existence, and that was in the print-and-whorl safe in Earlam's private office.

As secure as any system could be, and yet here was Agnew saying that they had to consider the question of a leak. The movements of certain shares possessed a significance that seemed too much for coincidence. So serious was Earlam taking it that he had called for an extraordinary meeting of the full board to discuss the matter. It was the first time in Maskell's experience that the directors had met other than at the normal three-monthly Doomsdays, as the stocktaking days were generally known.

If word of such a break in routine were to get out, Agnew said, it would inevitably lead to speculation and rumour that could do untold harm. So the meeting was to be held in some isolated place, site not yet decided, and under conditions of top security.

He finished explaining the situation, and the part Maskell was to play, in a few brief sentences.

"The meeting is provisionally scheduled for a week on Wednesday. You have a week in which to collate your general returns. The latest holdings figures will be in your hands next Monday, a week from today. It has been suggested that you leave that same day for the site of the meeting. This should allow you enough time in which to finalise your full report. It isn't necessary for me to ask you not to take anyone into your confidence, not even your personal staff. Everyone is under suspicion. You will, of course, travel alone. And by air, I think, if the site we have in mind is approved."

By air it had been, and to this, the last place under God's sun. Another of Agnew's country cottages? Maskell looked wryly about him. Hardly likely. What was more likely was that Saturn, through one of its satellites, had acquired a stretch of moorland for some reason or other—there wasn't oil in the Scottish Highlands, for God's sake?—and the house had been part of it.

And that was it. Agnew, always Agnew, had rung him at his flat last night telling him to be at Coventry by eleven the next morning, this morning. One of Agnew's private secretaries had been there to meet him with the papers containing the latest holdings figures. These, sorted and analysed, had to be melded with the information he had already collated—a week of hard work—and the complete picture made ready to put before the board when it met the day after tomorrow.

In a cold, dirty, barely furnished house, with no facilities worth mentioning, no staff, and no possible hope of the place being made even moderately habitable in time?

It didn't make sense. Something had obviously gone wrong somewhere; someone had slipped up badly over organising the thing. Not Agnew—that was unthinkable. Much as he disliked the man, with no good reason for that dislike, Maskell had to give him his due. Whatever Agnew undertook to do, he did with supreme efficiency.

Whatever he undertook to do . . . And into Maskell's mind came the sudden notion that perhaps nothing had gone wrong with the operation after all, that everything had gone according to some carefully worked-out plan, that it had been intended from the start that he be marooned—and that was the very word that came into his mind—marooned out here in the wilds. A moment of rising uneasiness brought coldness to the pit of his stomach as he sought desperately to think of Agnew's reasons for doing such a thing. Then the sensation melted as reason took over. He shook himself, angry with himself for the absurdity of such an idea; for here, no matter how inhospitable and lonely his surroundings might seem, he was only a stone's throw away from a village. A village with cottages and people, with a warm and comfortable public house; for where there is a church there is always a pub, and country pubs are always warm and welcoming places.

So it seemed that the only sensible possible explanation for his present predicament was that Agnew had entrusted part of the operation to one of his staff, and that underling had bungled, sending first the man Howard, then the helicopter, to the wrong place. Which meant the only course open to him now was to make the best of things until such times as the mistake had been discovered and rectified. And making the best of things certainly meant a drink in the village pub, followed by a hot meal, followed by a comfortable bed.

A few minutes before six, according to the grandfather clock with its bruised walnut panels and dial of engraved phases of the moon. Maskell checked with his own watch; it felt as though it should be later than that. But six was right, still early, but not too early to stroll down to the village to order dinner at the pub. He hoped they kept a respectable cellar. The few Scotsmen he knew were expert and authoritative drinkers and hearty trenchermen. And what did it feel like out-of-doors now?

It took him a few moments to master the complexity of a double-action handle. The sky, purpling now, was still cloudless. A V of birds, some kind of long-necked birds, moved steadily from one horizon to the other, keeping formation like a flight of planes. There were no sounds of any kind; it was perhaps the first time in his life he had come across such conditions of complete and utter silence. The small copse of unidentifiable trees flanking the drive on the left barely moved, so still was the air. The earlier chilly breeze seemed to have dropped, but it was still cold for someone not used to open spaces. Closing the door again—ugly indeed the blue and green stained glass—Maskell returned to his luggage, picking up the larger suitcase and taking it over to the seat of one of the hard-backed chairs against the wall.

As he had hoped, Judd had packed one of his overcoats, a double-breasted blue affair, warm enough, but certainly more at home in a city street than out on an open moor, where it would look somewhat ridiculous. But better, underneath was a thick, white turtlenecked pullover—bless old Juddy and his foresight—a pair of substantial flannels and a tweed jacket that he had bought in an on-the-spur moment and had never before found occasion to wear.

Returning the clothes to the case, he closed it and picked it up, tucked the briefcase of private papers under one arm and was reaching to pick up the second suitcase, about to carry the lot up to one of the bedrooms, when the phone rang, the un-expected sound making him jump.

And so why hadn't the idea of ringing Agnew occurred to him before, instead of having to wait for the phone itself to suggest the idea to him? Angry with himself for the second time in minutes, Maskell let his load drop to the floor. And straighten-ing, looking round in search of the source of the ringing, found the excuse that during his tour of the house he hadn't noticed a telephone. If he had seen it, he would have used the damn thing there and then. Subconsciously, he must have decided there wasn't one. But there was, and it was ringing away, almost cer-tainly with someone, probably Agnew, waiting to tell him that the mistake had been discovered and was being rectified.

So where was the instrument? The sound, perhaps because of the echo qualities of bare floors and little in the way of bulky fur-niture, seemed to come from no direction in particular. He tried first the room on the right, where the leather settee and easy chairs had earlier suggested a lounge. Nothing there, and no cup-boards or out-of-sight corners to investigate. So through into the room with the french windows. With the insistent ringing now seeming to come from somewhere above his head, he opened a small wall cupboard, found it empty and hurried through the door into the room on the right, this long and narrow, projecting outwards, making the house L-shaped. He had remarked it as being completely empty on his tour, but he made sure of it, and of the adjoining room also, desolately empty this, with strips of a long-ago blue willow-pattern paper hanging from brown-stained walls.

A door on the right took him back into the settee and chairs room. Through it, back into the hall, across to another skimpily furnished room, with twin cupboards built into the wall on each side of a large open stone fireplace. The ringing stopped abruptly in mid-pattern as he knelt to try the cupboards. A sense of grow-ing irritation gave way to small anger. What bloody fool had seen fit to hide a thing like a telephone in a place where it couldn't easily be found? One thing: whoever had been ringing would think he'd left the house for some reason, and would soon be back, and so they'd certainly ring again. And when they did, he promised himself, he'd know where to lay his hands on the damn thing.

He took his time over the search now. Not in the next room, and there he even rapped the wooden panels alongside its stone fireplace because he fancied they resembled a door. Back then into the hall, and another look there, a double check, because the hall was the most likely place. But nothing, and so into the kitchen, and some time spent opening every cupboard, eight of them and none empty, each holding cans—soups, vegetables, meat products, fruits—packets of biscuits, cereals. A door to the space under the sink wasn't worth the trouble of opening, but he made sure anyway, and even took time to take another look at the black monster range.

Not on the ground floor, he was positive of that, so back upstairs for a second tour of the bedrooms, this time looking in every corner, in every place where anything could be hidden. Some ten minutes later he walked slowly back along the gallery to the top of the stairs, frowning, trying to figure out the somewhat childish but nonetheless puzzling mystery of how one can hear a telephone ring when there is no telephone in the place.

Hands in his trouser pockets, he came down the stairs one pensive step at a time, mentally retracing his steps, wondering if there was anything, some odd corner, he might have missed. You will find the house confusing at first, Howard had said, but perhaps only for something to say; the only confusion Maskell had come across was that there were some rooms one could only reach by first having to pass through two others, and that only on the ground floor. Upstairs, by reason of the passage that was an extension of the gallery in both directions, every room was easily accessible.

No, he had missed nothing. But for having heard the damn thing ring he would have taken any odds against there being a phone in the house. Time would solve the mystery of some idiotic hiding place. In the meantime, the village pub would surely have one he could use. And at least one thing had come out of the fruitless search: he had come to know the place inside out.

Returning to his cases, about to pick them up again, he paused, staring at them. Something about the pattern they made gave the impression of their having been moved since he had last seen them. Imagination, of course, for he was alone in the house; that was one thing he could be sure of. But the impression persisted, then hardened. As he remembered that when the phone had rung he had dropped the cases he was holding, and hurried away, leaving them just as they were: the two briefcases untidily flanked by the suitcases. And now they were all neatly lined up, and the other way round, the suitcases in the middle.

They had been moved. His face grim, Maskell bent over the all-important briefcase, testing its lock, finding it intact. Relieved at least on that score, he straightened slowly, frowning thoughtfully now. There were no signs of any attempt having been made to force it open, and certainly nobody could have mastered the intricacies of its unique, complicated lock in the short time it had been left unattended. And now common sense pointed out that if the intruder, and it must have been an intruder, had been after the contents of that particular case, he would simply have taken it away with him. So that wasn't it. So who the hell in their right mind would force their way into a house and then apparently do nothing more than straighten out a line of luggage?

Force an entry . . . Maskell went over to the front door. It took only seconds to discover that for all the complications of its double-action handle, it worked equally well from the outside when the door was closed. Useful, bloody useful. No key, and no bolt, although he did notice screw marks where a bolt must have once been, but a long time ago if the condition of the marks was anything to go by. A trusting lot, the people who must once have lived here, God knows how many years ago.

At least it solved one problem that hadn't occurred to him until now: how to get back inside again, without a key, if the pub couldn't put him up, and he had to walk back here to rough it. He grimaced; that was a happy thought.

And as for the intruder . . . Some sort of village idiot, or the like, perhaps accustomed to having the run of the house through the years it had stood empty. Maskell shrugged. If he did have to spend the night here, a chair jammed under the handle would have to serve as a bolt.

Loaded, he struggled up the uncarpeted stairs to take over the furnished bedroom that showed no signs of recent occupancy. At least the bed linen was clean, if a little on the chill side, and damp to the touch. In the more modern bathroom of the two, stripped to the waist, he washed in brown-tinged water that was cold enough to make him catch his breath and so soft it felt like silk. Back in the bedroom, almost six-thirty by his watch on the cheap-looking deal dressing table, he put on flannels, pullover and tweed jacket. Combing his hair in the tarnished mirror he caught sight of the reflection of the two briefcases on the bed, and found another small problem to be solved.

By rights, he shouldn't let the case of important papers out of his sight. So what? So dressed like a country squire, in flannels and tweeds, he would go strolling through the village lugging a city briefcase. Ridiculous wouldn't be the word. He could see the yokels grinning. And apart from that, it was bulky and no light weight. But it would be a damn sight more ridiculous to leave it in a house with a front door that any passing tramp could open simply by turning the handle.

On the other hand—and he smiled sourly to himself at the no-tion—Howard, presumably it had been Howard—had managed to hide a telephone so effectively that it was impossible to find, even when shrilling its head off. In any event—a new idea; not used to having to fend for himself in this fashion, he was having to work things out as he went along—if he were to leave the case in some hiding place, it would only be for a short time either way. If the pub could find him a bed, he would still have to come back here to collect his things. The briefcase could then go back with him to the pub.

He found a hiding place of sorts in the older of the two bathrooms. Here, a sort of lid had been hinged to the wall in such a way it could be let down by a length of thick string—fairly new string by its appearance—to cover the bath and provide a shelf on which stuff could be stored. The sort of arrangement usually associated with cramped conditions. It was hard to imagine a past in which so much junk had accumulated in the house that they had found it necessary to rig up a gadget like this. To complete the boxed-in effect, another oblong of wood slotted along the front of the bath, which, when dropped down, revealed a space at the tap end just wide enough to take the briefcase on end. Maskell pushed it in, draped a piece of old cloth over it for good measure, and put the wood back into place. If anyone were to come specifically looking for the case, unlike the telephone they wouldn't have too much trouble finding it. But he had the feeling that the very last thing the folk in this God-forsaken place were interested in were sets of confidential company returns.

He remembered in time to pick up his watch on his way back downstairs. Fastening it to his wrist, he glanced automatically at the clock in the hall. Earlier, as dependable as the Bank of England, it had told the right time. Now, still going, its slow somnolent tick the only sound in the place, the scrollwork hands stood at half past four. Which meant—Maskell paused in the middle of adjusting it to the correct time—that it had either suddenly decided to go backwards, which didn't seem very likely, or else somebody had done what he was doing now, only pushing back instead of forward. The village idiot in action again. Tiptoe in, square up the luggage, put the clock back a couple of hours, tiptoe out again, a good day's work. The sooner a stop was put to those larks, the better.

He took another good look at the front door before opening it. A chair back jammed under a knob in a movie always worked. He had the feeling it might be less effective in real life, especially where the floor was stone-flagged. He hoped the necessity for barricading himself in wouldn't arise, that the pub would provide shelter until such times as Agnew got round to lifting him out.

If anything, it didn't seem quite so cold outside. He was wearing thicker clothes, of course, but it was the air itself that seemed milder. The sky was starting to cloud over, but there was nothing menacing or rain-promising about the gentle orange and pink billows that were building up along the horizon. A line of birds flapped in desultory fashion overhead. The sky never seemed empty of life out here. A flat world of great spaces and sweet air and wings.

Feeling in his pocket to make sure of his wallet, Maskell looked in the direction of the village as he walked along the moss-eroded drive towards the road. A mile away from the house, the pilot had read off from his map, but it seemed much closer than that, perhaps an illusion of clear air and absence of perspective. There were no gates dividing the drive from a road that was empty in both directions, only the hinges set in stone pillars where gates had once hung. A little-used road. Now, Maskell came to think, he couldn't recall having heard any vehicle sounds at all since his arrival. And it wasn't straight, as it had seemed when viewed from the house, but made up of a series of sweeping curves.

And another discovery: the ground which had seemed solid enough from the air turned out to be another illusion. Only minutes after leaving the house, the ground dipped on the left to give way to a black expanse of marsh, edged with reeds and rushes, and dotted with small islands of coarse grass. Mist was already starting to collect in the hollows. While the air at face level still felt comfortably warm, that now dankly seeping from both sides of the crumbling road was cold and penetrating.

There was a place where the road sank a little, so that banks of the coarse, sharp-edged grass grew shoulder-high on either side. In another place a small copse of trees must long ago have been swallowed by the mud, only bare bleached branches growing out from the patches of black ooze.

Maskell, walking more briskly now, looking forward to the comfort of the village, shivered a little at the loneliness of it all, an empty world, silent but for the occasional distant bird cry.

Another curve in the road, and now the village was beginning to take shape: a sizeable enough place so far as he could tell; cottages—that's all they'd be, cottages—grey walls and low grey roofs and grey chimneys that tapered to points. And not much height to any of it, no cottages taller than the rest, only the square, squat church tower, built of the same grey stone as the rest. Granite, he supposed. Wasn't that one of the favorite stones of Scotland?

And as he neared the village the ground seemed to become more solid on both sides of the road, edging the marsh away. Now there were patches of brownish bracken, gorse, clumps of heather. But still, in his eyes, a desolate wilderness. If this was Rannock Moor, the Scots were welcome to it. Not surprising he hadn't come across any of the villagers, out for an evening stroll. It couldn't be an inviting prospect, even to folk used to this sort of wild scenery.

He came to the first cottage: small and neat, made with a child's toy bricks; solid-looking front door, one tiny window on either side; no curtains, too early for a light to be on, and so looking to be empty, untenanted. And beyond, a group of three more, all alike; and then a row of them, rows on both sides of the widening road, with a tiny doll's shop. "McTavish. Hardware." And there, a short distance ahead, where the road divided, set in the triangle was a public-house sign, too far away yet for him to read the name. But there it was, as he had known it would be: drink and food and company, a telephone and, with some luck, a bed.

And then suddenly, quite suddenly, came the feeling that something was wrong. Nobody, not a single person to be seen. No animals. No sounds of any kind. No smoke from any of the cottage chimneys, no curtains at any of the cottage windows. No goods in any of the shop windows.

"The Highlander" the pub was called. A crude, garish painting of the inevitable kilted Highland warrior. Guarding a closed door and four more empty, curtainless windows. A crossroads, this; clearly the heart of the place. A patch of coarse grass, a crooked milestone, a tottering signpost: "Oban" in one direction, "Ballachulish" the other. Four roads of toy cottages with dead windows. A faded sign over cracked glass: "Kirkmalcolm Post Office." The door opened with an effort, grating over the floor. On dusty, musty emptiness; a hollow shell.

The whole village was a dusty, lifeless, hollow shell.

▒ THREE ▒

There was a bench on the triangle of grass, a crude affair of one long slab of uneven stone set across two smaller pieces. Maskell sat on it for a while, his back against the drunken signpost, three empty, lifeless roads there in front of him, another behind if he were to turn his head and look back the way he had come. The cold emptiness of it all was almost a tangible thing, a plague that had invaded him, making him part of itself.

At first he had refused to accept the obvious, trying one door after another, cottages and shops, none of them locked, all opening on to dusty bare rooms. No life in any of them, and the church perhaps the worst, an echoing empty shell, stripped of pews and pulpit and altar, shadows in far corners, thin bars of colour reflected from stained glass and laid across the dusty boards.

And the reason for all this? A mock-up; that was the first thought that came to mind. A village built for some movie or other. But the church, if nothing else, discounted that theory, with the marks on the floor where the furnishings had been ripped out. This place was for real. No clapboard and false frontages. Services had been held in the centuries-old church: christenings, marriages, funerals. Funerals . . . He had found a graveyard at the back, but no headstones that he could see, barred from actually entering by a barrier of briar and gorse.

A real place and, yes, he remembered, it had been marked on the helicopter pilot's map. He wished he'd paid more attention to it now. People had lived here, and then one day they'd packed up and left. But not in any kind of panic, because people in a hurry to get away wouldn't waste time uprooting the pews and all the other stuff from the church to take away with them. A careful, orderly exodus, this had been. But trying to figure out the whys and wherefores wasn't going to help him now.

Maskell looked at his watch, twenty past seven, and pushed himself a little stiffly to his feet; the bench had been very hard. In the city there would be another hour of daylight left; out here, in the open spaces, perhaps a little more. As well to get back to the house while it was still light. It seemed he had no choice but to spend the night there. He grimaced; after a scratch meal, with the briefcase under his pillow and the front door barricaded to put a stop to the village idiot's perambulations.

And then another thought. Where does your village idiot come from when there isn't a village? There was this place, the house, and not another building of any kind in sight for miles. There was only one answer: all the cottages here might seem to be empty, but one of them wasn't. Somebody was living in one of them. Maskell shrugged. So what. So good luck to him, and a thick ear if I catch him fooling about with my stuff again.

He set off on the return journey, dispirited, gloomy, not looking forward in any way to what lay ahead. Preoccupied with the imagined discomforts of the immediate future, oblivious to everything else, it was some little time before another thought came, this one striking him so forcibly it brought him to a halt.

Earlier, he had set aside the notion of his having been deliberately isolated out here—"marooned," that had been the word —because how could one be in any way cut off from things with a village within stone's throw? But there was no cosy little village standing helpfully by. There was damn all. From where he stood now, he could see clear to the horizon on all sides, God knows how many miles away that was, and while the land wasn't exactly flat, there didn't seem to be any hills or hillocks, or whatever they called the bloody things out here, pronounced enough to hide any kind of building.

It did seem, on the face of it, that he was virtually isolated. Deliberately arranged, or a blunder on someone's part? If a mistake, then it was just sheer bad luck that of all the places to choose from, the blunderer had picked what must certainly be one of the very few places in the country where complete isolation could be achieved. And that, Maskell told himself grimly, was the sort of coincidence he didn't go for.

He resumed walking, slowly now, gaze remote, trying to work out the motive for what had been done to him. It was as clear as day who was behind it. For some reason or other, Agnew had wanted him out of circulation. Not Maskell the man, for with Agnew personalities counted for nothing, but Maskell of Forward Projection and Clear Intention.

Something in the way of share manipulation. That was a fairly safe bet. And big, big as they come, for Agnew to jeopardise his top-of-the-heap status. Maskell nibbled pensively on his lower lip as he wondered just how long it was intended he be kept out of the way. He could forget about the board meeting the day after tomorrow; that had been nothing more than an excuse to get him out here. There might be an indication in the amount of food in the kitchen cupboards. Two weeks at least, he estimated, mentally reviewing the stacked shelves, possibly longer.

It was hardly likely, he felt, that any others of his staff had been similarly shunted out of sight. Too many sudden absences would cause comment. In any case, they'd probably have ended up here too if Agnew had sorted any of them out.

Just dumped out here in the wilds with no regard for comfort, feelings, personal inconvenience. You'd treat an animal with more consideration. Maskell fought against a surge of anger. Whatever happened, he must keep his head. Working up a lather wasn't going to help him any. Neither was thinking of what he'd do or say to Agnew next time they came face to face. He grimaced to himself. It was unlikely the two of them would ever meet again. Unless he were to take a trip to South America, which was where people who make illicit fortunes usually take themselves.

A sudden breeze stirred the tall grass and was cold on his face. He quickened his pace. It would soon be getting dark. There was little or nothing he could do tonight about getting away from here. With no notion at all of the geography of this part of the world, he hadn't the slightest idea how far away the nearest place of any size might be. Oban. Or—what had that other outlandish name been on the signpost? Bally—something or other. Ballachulish. And how far away was the nearer of these likely to be? Say, fifteen to twenty miles at the outside. A damned long walk, but not impossible by any means. Maskell smiled grimly. He'd do it if it were twice that distance, if for nothing more than the pleasure of seeing Agnew's face. So on the agenda for tomorrow, one route march.

And in the meantime he wasn't as entirely cut off as perhaps Agnew had bargained for. There was still the telephone in the house, that's if he could find the bloody thing. And why had it been hidden so effectively? There had to be a reason for that, and for why Agnew didn't know about a link with the outside world that made nonsense of his whole plan of isolation. The only answer was that the phone had only recently been installed, and hidden, just to be on the safe side. By Howard, perhaps, but why, and under whose instructions, didn't much matter for the time being. But for the record, and Maskell was pleased with the deduction, by somebody with influence. Assuming there hadn't been a telephone in the house before, it must have taken some doing persuading the post office to bring one all the way out here. Miles of posts and wire . . . And where were they? A telegraph pole out here, just one within miles, would stick out like a sore thumb, never mind a whole line of them, marching back across these bloody marshes to civilisation. There was nothing even faintly resembling a telegraph pole to be seen.

Maskell turned in through the twin pillars guarding the drive. The method used to bring the wires to the house wasn't important. All that mattered was that they had been brought, and the phone was working. He fumbled with the door handle, momentarily forgetful of its double action, opened it and stepped into the comparative warmth of the hall. His luggage, all of the cases except for one briefcase, were arranged in a careful row in the very centre of the stone floor.

The village idiot in action again. Lips compressed, Maskell shook his head. Innocent enough it might all be, childish, but damned annoying. But annoyance tempered with the feeling that it was nice to know he wasn't alone out here, even though his invisible companion was on the queer side. He tested the weight of the cases. By the feel, everything had been repacked. He didn't relish the thought of strange hands pawing through his things. He glanced across at the clock. Quarter to five, it told him, while he knew without having to consult his own watch that it must be getting on for eight. In a way, there was a kind of reason about the repacking of the cases and bringing them downstairs again to convey a message. "Go away from here and leave the house to me again." But he could see no sense of any kind in this continual altering of the time.

Maskell carried the cases back up to his chosen bedroom again and left them there while he went on a quick tour of inspection to make sure his visitor had left. Back in the hall he jammed the back of one of the chairs under the front-door handle, tested it and was fairly satisfied it would stand up at least to any normal attempt to open it from the outside. He examined each of the french windows, shook his head ruefully at the absence of bolts and locks, tried jamming one of the catches with a sliver of wood, and gave it up as a hopeless job. Whoever the people were who'd once lived here, they certainly hadn't been burglar-conscious.

A faint purpling of the sky was a reminder that dusk wasn't far away. He became aware of feeling hungry. The last time he had eaten had been in Coventry, a scratch meal at the tiny airfield buffet. He grimaced. At least he hadn't had to prepare it himself. In the kitchen he eyed the black monster with distaste. If he wanted something hot to eat and drink then he'd have to do something about bringing the thing to life. There were ashes in the grate; two saucepans and a frying pan upside down on a metal grille; teapot at one side, kettle the other. By the look of it, Howard had also had to do his own catering. A lidless cardboard carton in one corner of the room served as waste bin. Its empty cans suggested Howard had existed on an unimaginative but perhaps "Hobson's choice" diet of beans, sausages and rice pudding. But at least he had cleaned up after himself. The adequate selection of crockery in one of the cupboards had been washed and stacked. A wooden box contained knives, forks and spoons, and a very essential can opener. There were firewood and newspapers in one of the ovens, coal in a tarnished copper scuttle and boxes of matches in one of the cupboards. Maskell took off his jacket and rolled up his sleeves.

A thought came to him, sometime later, as he crouched in front of his carefully laid fire, watching the flames take hold. His hands still black with coal dust, he went out into the hall and upstairs, first to where he had hidden the briefcase of private papers, still safe where he had left it, then along the darkening passage with it to his bedroom, to unlock it with the key attached by a chain to his flannel trousers.

It contained what it was supposed to contain, the latest data on all Saturn companies, and not, as he had for a moment thought, a pile of any old rubbish. Which meant Agnew was taking a risk. He frowned down at them, the top sheet stamped with his black thumbprint. Once he had collated and correlated the information contained in these papers with that in those in the other case, any sizeable trend in share movement would show up. Nothing precise, for the vital figures would all be in code, but proof enough to anyone with experience of what Agnew was up to.

And yet these papers had been allowed to reach the one man most likely to read significance in them. Not a mistake; Agnew, who never made mistakes anyway, wouldn't have dropped a clanger like that. Allowed to reach Maskell because he was so sure he couldn't do anything about it until it was too late? Perhaps, but risky; nothing is certain. And then Maskell suddenly saw how Agnew could have had no choice but to let the papers through, untouched. There was always the possibility that Maskell would have started work on them while in the helicopter. Anything remotely fishy, and the 'copter would have been ordered back by its passenger. That was it; he could be sure these were the genuine returns, and the sooner he started work on them to get the picture of what was going on, the better. Eat first, work after. Maskell pushed the papers back into the case, locked it and carried it back down with him to the kitchen, where the fire blazed brightly in the gathering dusk.

He selected cans and opened a packet of unsweetened biscuits, obviously a substitute for bread. Instant coffee, evaporated milk.

The last time he had done this sort of thing—the only time in his life, now he came to think—was at a Boy Scout camp when he was fourteen. A novelty then, and, the best way of looking at it, a novelty now. A matter of refusing to let the primitive conditions get the better of him, instead of making the best of things until he could get away.

The telephone rang as he was filling the kettle, the sound, as before, seeming to come from no direction in particular. It was certainly no clearer in the hall. But it did seem to get louder as, head cocked, kettle still in hand, he mounted the stairs. If anything, it got fainter as he tried tracking it along the passage past his bedroom, grew louder again when he turned in the opposite direction, seeming now to come from the unlikely source of the two bathrooms at the far end of the lefthand passage. The ringing stopped, in mid-peal as before, as he opened the door of the bathroom where he had earlier hidden the case. The only place where anything of any size could be concealed was under the bath itself, and that space was now completely empty.

It would be waste of time to pursue the search in this half-light. Back in the kitchen he put the kettle on the fire and set about opening cans and tipping out their contents. Soup, macaroni and cheese, fruit pudding. A more imaginative approach than his predecessor had shown. He sorted out cutlery, laid a place at the deal table, went to the door to switch on the light. It was only when nothing happened that he found the light socket empty. Another quick tour of the place brought not a single light bulb; every socket in every room was empty.

It appeared, then, that the two old-fashioned and ornate copper and brass oil lamps—one in the room with the leather suite, the other here in the kitchen—which he had taken to be purely and trendily ornamental, were after all very much utilitarian. Grimacing distaste at the smell when he removed the glass globe, this the first time he had ever tackled an oil lamp, it took him a few minutes to master the flaring and smoke of the wick. When it was alight, he brought the other one, adding its light to the first in an attempt to make the room look cheerful. And turning from setting it on the table, he fancied he saw something at the window over the sink, a flicker of movement in one of the dark panes, the vague impression of a white oval that imagination could have turned into a face pressed to glass if reason hadn't suggested that it was nothing more than the reflection of the first oil lamp, now on the shelf over the range.

When he had finished eating, Maskell piled all his dirty things in the sink, a little surprised at the number he had used, made a cup of coffee and took it and one of the lamps through to the lounge, which he supposed was the purpose of the room with the settee and easy chairs, returning for his briefcase and the other lamp. It was cold now after the warmth of the kitchen fire, but he wasn't accustomed to working in the same room in which he had eaten, with the smell of food still there, and he didn't intend starting now. He discovered the inconvenience of having to carry his own light with him when he returned to the kitchen to collect paper, firewood and coal, and have second thoughts about the box of matches, exchanging it for a shovelful of glowing embers and a precarious, spark-drifting journey across the hall and to the lounge fireplace.

And squatting in front of his ready-made fire, nursing it through its first few minutes, he remembered the whitish oval he had seen at the window and taken to be the lamp's reflection because that had seemed the most reasonable explanation. But now, thinking back, it could equally well have been a face, that of the luggage-shifting, time-altering village idiot. He shrugged, hands on the stone floor on either side of him. With most of the window catches faulty, there wasn't much hope of preventing any intruders from getting into the house if they had their minds set on it. At least this one intruder didn't seem out to do any harm.

Maskell took one of the lamps up to his bedroom to collect the other briefcase. Then he pulled the settee closer to the fire, unlocked both cases and laid out their contents on a coffee table brought from the other side of the room. Still standing, he was already studying the first sheet as he rolled down his sleeves and reached for the jacket he had thrown over the back of the settee. From the contents of the first case he took a sheaf of fresh paper and three pens. Then he sat down and was lost to the world.

Sometime later the clatter of the fire collapsing in the grate brought him back from his private world of figures and précis assessments. Almost nine o'clock. Bright moonlight outside, when he went to the window; hazing the distance, drifting across the drive, pooling under the bushes and trees. He went to the kitchen for more coal, lugging the heavy scuttle back with him to save wasting time over several journeys with the toy shovel. Sitting down again, he resumed work. The phone rang, automatically bringing him to his feet. But if he hadn't been able to track it down in broad daylight, he didn't stand much chance now. Lowering himself to his seat, he picked up his pen and bent over the papers. After a while the ringing stopped.

When the fire died down for the second time he let it stay that way. Almost eleven now, and the best part of three hours' hard graft under his belt. Hard indeed, and with not a thing to show. Everything honest and aboveboard. Or so it seemed. Nothing positive that he could set his finger on. Not a shred of suspicion. But it was there, he could sense it, but so skilfully camouflaged as to defy expert scrutiny. Disappointing; frustrating. But so far he had only skimmed the surface. There was much more still to be done. And somewhere he would find it, because he knew it was there.

He leaned back, stretching, yawning, rubbing the outer corners of his eyes with his fingertips. Somewhere, quite close, a man's voice said something, the words indistinguishable; another voice answered, a soft muttering of syllables. On his feet, Maskell ran out into the hall. The voices still spoke together in the darkness, their wordless sibilant mutterings, like that of the telephone ringing, seeming to come from no direction in particular. He hurried back into the lounge to snatch up one of the lamps and return with it, flame flaring, to dispel only some of the shadows. His chair, for what it was worth, was still jammed under the front-door handle. When he stood by it, the voices were certainly inside the house, not coming from beyond the door. They seemed to get louder, but no clearer, when he stood at the foot of the stairs. He was halfway up, lamp held over his head, when the sounds stopped. For perhaps a minute he stood looking up into the darkness of the gallery, listening, waiting for it to start again. When it didn't, when everywhere remained silent, he came slowly back down into the hall and across to the lounge.

The fire was almost out, but it had become comfortably warm in the room. He was getting tired—he turned from setting the lamp on the mantelpiece—but surely not tired enough to have only imagined those voices. What was more likely was that he had put the wrong construction on some other very ordinary night sound, perhaps rustlings in an empty place that had magnified and distorted the sound. Birds in the loft—owls would they be?—something like that.

He yawned hugely as he sat down again. Perhaps another hour of work and he would call it a day. He took the next sheaf of stapled papers from the pile. Mather, he noted automatically, one of the smaller concerns; electronics. He flicked through the first pages, not concerned with their contents for the time being, only requiring to read the collected final reports from the chairman and managing director. Both margins and the top and bottom of that page of typing and columns of coded figures were filled with pencilled calculations done in a wavering, spidery hand. It took only seconds for him to realise just what those calculations were: the pencilled figures were coded returns decoded. Somebody, one of three men, Agnew, Brownlea or Earlam himself, had for some reason or other, reproduced in clear the returns, or some of the returns, of one small and obscure company. And having done that, and presumably returned the code itself to its place of safety, had made the mistake of allowing that page of calculations to remain as it was instead of either erasing the pencillings or removing the sheet altogether.

Who was guilty, and what it had all been about, didn't matter at the moment. What was important was that now, with this information, incomplete as it was, in front of him, it should be possible, by a system of trial and error, to work out the code in full. And then, having done that, apply it to all the four-hundred-odd Bluesheets here in his possession, and so end up with a detailed and accurate picture of what had been going on. Instead of suspicions of Agnew, he would have firm proof.

Filled with a sense of exhilaration, Maskell bent over the columns of pencilled figures and letters. Without taking his eyes from them, he wiped his sticky palms with his handkerchief, picked up his pen and drew a fresh sheet of paper towards him. His tiredness was forgotten. When, sometime later, he did lay his pen down and lean back, it wasn't because he was unable to continue working but because he had discovered that the task he had set himself had turned out to be much more complicated than he had first thought, that the code was infinitely more complex than he had ever imagined. Even with the calculations as a basis to work on, it was still very much a hit-and-miss affair, with no shortcuts. Time-consuming, and for all he knew there might be very little time left before Agnew caused Saturn irreparable damage. He weighed one course against another: whether to continue work on the code, or go back to his original collating of general assessments in the hope that something positive would emerge.

Debating the problem, he leaned back, closing his eyes. The pen slipped from his fingers. He fell asleep. And after a while he had a dream.

He dreamed that something—a sound of which he was only vaguely aware, a distant throbbing—woke him, and he rose from the settee and went to the window to look outside. Moonlight filled the silent world. Tentacles of mist drifted eerily from the shadows of the small copse of trees. Something seemed to move in front of that dark frieze of motionless branches. Shadows coiled and gathered and took shape. The two figures that stood there looked to be real and solid, but even in his dream Maskell was able to reason out that they were too incredible in those surroundings to be flesh and blood.

The man was tall and distinguished-looking, impressive in bearing, almost dominating, certainly somebody of importance. In his fifties, Maskell's dream-self judged. Bareheaded, his dark hair seemed to be plastered down across an unusually broad forehead, arranged in a series of flat curls. He wore—at midnight, in that place of mists and marsh—he wore full evening regalia of white tie and dress suit. The jewels of some decoration glittered on his white shirt front. His black cloak, long and theatrical, was clasped at the throat with a metal chain and thrown back to expose its vivid scarlet lining.

And the woman . . . younger than her companion, it seemed to Maskell in his dream, for all her features weren't clearly visible beneath the deep forehead fringe of light-coloured hair. And like the man, dressed for some special occasion. In her case, for some unimaginable occasion. She wore what could have been some sort of masquerade costume—scarlet, form-hugging silk that even in that light sparkled with sequins. It left her shoulders and most of her breasts exposed; gleaming white alabaster rising out of sleek scarlet silk. And no skirt of any kind, her long slender black-silk legs exposed from ankles to rounded thighs.

Figures in a fantasy. Grotesque, in misty moonlight.

In his dream, Maskell pressed his face against the cold glass of the window.

The woman's head moved. She was looking straight towards him. She saw him; it was impossible for her not to see him. Maskell narrowed his eyes, straining without success to make out her features. She touched the man's arm, and in stately manner he inclined his massive head with its unnatural curls to hear what she was saying. Her hand still on his arm, together they turned, walked away, melted into the mists. And in his dream, Maskell turned away from the window, paused by the lamp on the table to turn it out—that on the mantelpiece was already out—then returned to the settee, laid his head on the cold leather back again and went back to sleep.

It was broad daylight when he woke. Well used to strange waking surroundings, never a heavy sleeper at any time, he never had any trouble orientating himself when waking in a morning. Now, on his feet, stretching, stiff after the night spent fully dressed on the cushionless, not overcomfortable settee, he was able to remember immediately where he was and what was going on.

Only nine-thirty, according to his watch. Late for him, but after last night's long working session he was lucky it wasn't even later. Stripping off his pullover and vest, he stopped by the mirror over the fireplace to inspect his overnight beard and hope that Judd had thought to pack his battery electric razor. Oddly, it was the sight of the lamp on the mantelpiece that brought back the dream. In his dream it hadn't been alight, although both it and the one on the table must still have been burning when he dropped off to sleep over his work. He could see now from the glass reservoir that it had run out of oil. Which meant that if he was still here tonight, which God forbid, he would have the messy job of filling it and trimming the charred wick. Of filling both of them, for the one on the table must also have burned itself dry during the night.

But its reservoir was half full, and the wick not charred but turned down. In his dream he had turned it down . . . Maskell turned to stare at the window, the centre one of the three where he had stood in the dream to watch the impossible people. There was something white on the floor by that window. A piece of crumpled paper, he thought at first. And then saw that it was his handkerchief, and he remembered using it last night to wipe his hands, and then had let it fall to his lap. And then, caught in the creases of his pullover, he must have carried it with him when he went to the window.

Not a dream. He had actually stood looking out of that window.

FOUR

More asleep than awake he had peered owlishly out into the night and taken moonlight and shadow and trees and made people of them. There wasn't a moment's doubt in his mind that he had only imagined the fantasy figures. That they might be real was too ridiculous. It was somewhat worrying, though, when one's mind played tricks of that kind, and why in heaven's name had it chosen such preposterous characters? Dracula, as ever he was; and attendant lady vampire, by courtesy of any fourth-rate horror epic. Or Batwoman, straight out of the comic strips. Or Mata Hari, a nice thought, but doubtful she'd ever gone in for a get-up of that kind.

Maskell, contemplating the scene of the imaginary visitation, smiled wryly to himself as he imagined what kind of psychiatric interpretations the great and wise Sir John Mellish-Rae would likely find to fit such bizarre imaginings. A yearning for lost childhood; a rejection of things normal. Or maybe, thinking in terms of bloodsucking and espionage, a rejection of high finance itself.

He went upstairs to wash and, noting the absence of any power point in the bathroom, mentally thanked Judd for having packed both mains and battery razors. He was hungry, he discovered with some surprise, more hungry, particularly at this time of day, than he had been in a long time. Possibly the replacing of city fumes by moorland freshness; more likely the outcome of the nonlasting properties of last night's scratch meal. Breakfast would have to be taken more seriously. Bacon there was, if only in cans. No eggs; no fresh food of any kind, come to that, and biscuits were a damn poor substitute for bread. He put on his jacket, remembered there was a grate to clean out, a fire to light and a sink full of dirty dishes to deal with, said "damn" under his breath and took the jacket off again, rolling up his pullover sleeves as he went down the stairs.

The voices came again as he reached the sunlit hall. And they were unmistakably human voices, no question this time of birds rustling in lofts. Men talking, two men at least, the words almost but not quite intelligible, irritatingly just out of reach. And with an odd kind of hollow, resonant quality, like men whispering with their faces close to the curved walls of a long empty tunnel, the sound near to and remote at the same time. Maskell called loudly: "Who's there?" and went quickly back up the stairs, calling again when he reached the gallery, then listening, head cocked, trying at the same time to pick out words and trace the direction they were coming from.

But as it had been with the telephone, the sound seemed to come from all directions, from no direction. If he had to choose, he would say the bathrooms again. The voices stopped as he entered the bathroom he had been using. Empty, of course, and he turned to look back along the passage, angry as well as puzzled, demanding aloud: "What the hell's going on?" There was no reply; he hadn't expected one. And when he went quickly through the house he knew the result would be like the other times. Nothing, nobody, no place where anyone or anything could be hidden. Perhaps something to do with acoustics, he thought; with his imagination working overtime again, but knew that couldn't be it, there had to be more to it than that.

A telephone rings when there is no phone there; men talk together and there is nobody there. Luggage packs itself and moves about, and for good measure a clock goes backwards. And two impossible people stand quietly in the moonlight. And what would Sir John have to say about that little lot?

Maskell went slowly down the stairs to take his chair from under the front-door handle, open the door and look out at the hazy morning of moorland and marsh and pale-blue sky. Birds hovering; rushes and branches stirring; the deception of church tower and cottage roofs. He was alone in the house; he might almost be alone in the world.

Drugs, he wondered; was that how it was being done? That

would account for his seeing and hearing things that weren't there. Bring him here, leave him alone, then change his world into a place without rhyme or reason. Disorientation. That sort of thing was done; he'd read about it, but only in the almost make-believe world of espionage and spies and agents. It didn't happen to men whose only concern was with columns of figures and company statements.

Closing the door he stood for a while looking round the hall. The clock, he noted in passing, was for once telling the right time.

Not drugs, he decided, for his senses were in no way blunted. He didn't think it likely a man could suffer drug-induced hallucinations one minute and be completely clear in his mind the next. There would surely be a persistent wooliness, a permanent, noticeable dulling of perceptions. Not drugs; something else.

And for what? There had to be a reason for what was being done to him. Arouse his suspicions that an attempt is being made to swindle Saturn; put into his hands the means of confirming those suspicions, then confuse him so that he is unable to concentrate upon what must be done. That seemed to be the general picture. It made sense of a sort, at a stretch of imagination. A damned long stretch. The only thing to do was ignore, try to ignore, the interruptions, the diversions, and not waste time trying to track them down or find explanations for them. Concentrate to the exclusion of all else on unearthing the proof of what Agnew was up to.

Maskell went through to the kitchen. Earlier, on his hurried tour, he had ignored the sink and its unwholesome load of dirty dishes and pans. Now that was something that would have to be tackled before getting breakfast. Hot water would be needed to deal with the clotted grease. He took the kettle over to the sink. To the now empty sink. Empty, and sparkling as much as chipped yellow stone could be said to sparkle. Its contents had been washed and dried and even, in the case of the saucepans, seemingly polished, and put back on the shelves.

But not stacked in the ordinary way in which crockery is stored, but arranged, even displayed, in a strange kind of maniac pattern: inverted plate balanced on inverted cup, another cup on top, larger plate on top again. No two saucers together; no two of anything similar together. The glistening knives, forks and spoons, laid out on the draining board, carried the same weird pattern. Arranged imbalance, yet with a kind of overall rhythmic effect. Haphazard in the extreme, and yet at the same time giving the impression that time and care had been taken to perfect the thing.

There was no way of telling when it had been done. This morning, probably, early. The village idiot yet again, and Maskell, already accustomed to the notion of sharing his temporary home with an invisible companion who seemed able to come and go at will, was more grateful for having had what was for him an unpleasant chore taken off his hands than annoyed by the intrusion.

"You could have cleaned the grate out at the same time," he observed, eyeing the mess of cold ash and cinders. And it was only when he heard the echo-sound of his own voice he realised he had spoken aloud. So now he had started talking to himself. A sign that all this was beginning to get through to him. That he should ever have considered the idea of drugs having been used on him, seriously considered such an idea, showed what state of mind he was in, that he hadn't come far from losing his sense of proportion. Everything that had happened since his arrival had been caused by purely mechanical means. Nothing supernatural, nothing hallucinatory. A series of not particularly sophisticated attempts to disturb his mental balance or perhaps scare him away from the place.

Before starting on the grate, Maskell went to the lounge to gather his papers together, return them to the two briefcases and bring them back to the kitchen where he could keep an eye on them. Then on hands and knees he set about raking out the ashes and laying a new fire.

The voices started again as he was opening a can of bacon. Opener in hand, he stood in the doorway, listening, able by concentrating to pick up a word here and there, but as before, unable to make any sense of it. When it stopped, the house seemed all the more silent by contrast. He thought about the sound that had woken him during the night. A throbbing, pulsating sound as he recalled, with something vaguely familiar about it. Only faint, and getting fainter, but at one time it must have been loud enough to break into his sleep. Intended deliberately to wake him and bring him to the window to see the prearranged charade? Possible, he supposed; but what guarantee would the originator have that his victim would indeed wake up, and having done so, get up and go to the window?

Obviously none at all, and so the moonlight show couldn't have been staged specially for his benefit. Which meant that his earlier idea, one he hadn't much cared for, had to be right after all. He had started seeing things that weren't there.

When he had finished breakfast he tumbled the dirty things in the sink. If the village idiot or whatever wanted to repeat his performance, he was more than welcome, so long as he stayed out of the way. But what kind of person, for God's sake, would make such an efficient job of the washing itself, then take time to stack the clean things in such a weird, unnatural fashion?

A briefcase in each hand, Maskell returned to the lounge and his coffee-table desk. For a while he brooded over the many pages of last night's abortive attempts at code-breaking. The light of the new day hadn't changed anything, had brought no new ideas. He had to accept that while the pencilled calculations were sufficient in themselves to form the basis on which to break down the code, there was only one way of going about it, and that way could take a very long time. A computer could cut days or weeks down to mere hours. A computer out here . . . That was a laugh.

So there was nothing for it but to return to his original careful scrutinising of general returns and reports until whatever he was looking for materialised. Which, given time—time again—it was bound to. He moved the table and one of the easy chairs over to the window where he could keep a not very optimistic eye on the road along which he had seen nothing or no one pass since his arrival. It was warm enough without a fire if he closed the door to the hall to cut off the draught. He looked at his watch; a few minutes before ten. If he hadn't come up with anything by twelve he'd call it a day, get a last meal and set off to find the nearest telephone.

He bent over the papers. The house was silent. Time slipped by. The small sound that made him look up didn't come from the direction of the kitchen as he first fancied, but was the rustling of the small clump of trees across the drive from his window, stirred by the breeze that must have sprung up. In the moment of focussing his eyes after their unbroken hour of concentration upon columns of small print, it seemed to catch a flicker of movement in the shadows of the same place where he had imagined the two figures. To go out and check would, he told himself, be pandering to that imagination and be so much wasted time.

The voices came again as he bent back over the papers. An oddly penetrating sound, for all its sense of hollowed remoteness, impossible to ignore. He leaned back, looking up at the dusty yellow plaster of the ceiling, knowing from before that it would be no use trying to track it down to its source. After a few seconds the voices faded away. And as he made to return to his work, he caught another stir of movement, this time not his imagination. Over on the right, the bushes that filled the triangle between drive and road were agitated, obviously being furiously shaken by someone or something. A tall, thin sapling branch reared up, fell sideways and separated itself from the rest, gripped in the hand of the man who now came into sight as he straightened up and stepped back. Holding his trophy in front of him he used a broad-bladed knife to hack off the top and trim away the side branches. Then he tested the firmness of his home-made pole by banging it sharply on the road.

Maskell came to life. His window, he found, was too stiff to open. He rapped on the glass, but the man in the road was seemingly too busy adjusting the straps of his macintosh-covered pack to hear. Maskell hurried into the hall, opened the front door, and his shout was just in time to catch the stranger as he passed by the drive entrance.

This time he did hear, looked round for the sound, found

where it had come from and was mouth-gapingly startled. Maskell caught the words: "Well, I'm bloody-well damned." Then the man was coming quickly along the drive towards him.

Tall, and younger than Maskell had first thought, seeing him from a distance. Not much more than thirty, he judged, and with a whitish face so long and narrow and squashed-looking as to smack of abnormality. His dark eyes slanted sideways and down, and were heavy-lidded at the outer corners. At first sight, not an intelligent-looking face by any means—that perhaps an impression suggested by the partly open mouth and drooping, thick lower lip. But that impression could easily be a misleading one. Certainly there was nothing oafish or dull about his alert, appraising gaze. Hatless, his thick black hair didn't appear to have seen a comb in weeks. He wore a crumpled grey high-necked sweater and grey slacks. And his smile, now he was over his startlement, was a very pleasant affair. He was clearly and unashamedly delighted, perhaps even relieved, by the encounter.

"I was going on past—" He motioned with his new stick. "I mean, I wasn't even bothering. Empty, I thought. I mean, well, it looked empty when I saw the place from back yonder, and after that bloody village. . . . Well, I didn't think for one moment there'd be anyone *living* here.

"Mate," he finished with great feeling, "you don't know how glad I am to see you."

"I'm equally glad to see you," Maskell assured him, and stepped aside. "You'd better come in."

"Ta." The other looked round the hall. "Christ. What time does the ghost walk?" Unhooking his arms from the straps he let his pack fall to the stone floor. "That's better. Fairfield." He offered his hand. "Bernard Fairfield. Don't say you live here?"

"I won't." Maskell shook the not overclean hand. "Boyd Maskell. What are you doing out here?"

"You might well bloody ask," Fairfield replied with some bitterness, and jerked his narrow head at his discarded pack. "Holiday. Some bleeding holiday. Got talked into it; you know how it is. Healthy; that sort of jazz. Thumbing lifts; sleeping rough; back to nature. The last bloody time, mate. You ever tried it?"

Maskell smiled a little. "When I was young. Boy Scouts."

"Ay. Bugger that for a lark, too. Don't say you're on holiday, too?"

"I won't," Maskell said, and pointed to the open door of the lounge. "There are some decent chairs in there. I was just going to make some coffee."

"Go down a fair treat," the other said with enthusiasm. "Want any help?"

"No," Maskell said, then changed his mind. "The fire might need stirring up."

In the kitchen the sink was empty and shining, the dishes washed and set back on the shelves in the same insane pattern as before. And all done while he had been working in the other room, not a dozen yards away.

"God Almighty," Fairfield breathed, eyeing the monster range. And then caught Maskell's expression. "What's the matter? Something up?"

"No," Maskell told him, and then changed his mind for a second time. "The village idiot in action," he said. "I came here yesterday. I'm alone here. I made breakfast; piled all the dirty things in the sink there; left them like that—oh—little more than an hour ago. And while I was away, as you can see, all washed and put away. The same thing happened with last night's dinner dishes. They were washed up sometime during the night."

"You're kidding." Fairfield looked hard at the empty sink. "You mean, someone you don't know about comes in when you're not looking and cleans up after you?" He transferred his gaze to the shelves. "And then sets them all out like that?"

"It's useful, of course," Maskell said. "Saves me a lot of trouble. I think I'd feel happier if I knew who it was, though."

"Fairies." The other's humour seemed somewhat forced. "You never know what you're likely to come across in places like these. Leprechauns. No, that's Ireland. Elves. The little folk." By his tone he didn't seem inclined to believe Maskell's story. He turned back to the range. "This all you got to do your brewing-up on?"

"It does the job." Maskell collected two cups and two saucers from various parts of the display, two teaspoons from the neat but asymmetrical ranks on the draining board.

"Christ," said Fairfield from the cupboards. "You got enough grub here to feed an army. Not much variety, though." He went to crouch on his haunches in front of the grate. "Wood?" He found it without any help. "You say you're not here on holiday?"

"It's a long story," Maskell said, opening a jar of instant coffee. "I'm hoping to get away later on today, round about twelve. It'll mean walking. I don't have a car."

Fairfield turned from feeding wood between the grate bars. "So where will you make for?" he wanted to know. "Where's the nearest town?"

Maskell looked up quickly, opener poised over can of milk. "Don't you know?" he asked abruptly.

The other leaned his shoulder against the oven door. "Of course I don't bloody know. I'm bloody lost. I don't know where I am or where I'm bloody going. Why the hell did you think I was so bloody pleased to find someone living in this bloody hole?"

Anxiety and disbelief sharpened Maskell's tone. "But God damn it, man, you *must* know. You say you walked here. So where was the last place you passed through?"

"Kirkmalcolm," Fairfield rejoined equally sharply. "And a fat lot of joy you'll get there, let me tell you. A bleeding ghost town. So what about you? You say you don't have a car, so you must have come on foot."

"By air." Maskell slowly finished opening the can of milk. "Helicopter."

"Christ." Fairfield pushed himself upright from the now blazing fire. "Just like that." He mimicked Maskell's precise voice. "By air. Well, let me tell you how I got here, mate. I was talked into this bloody hiking holiday by the bastards in the office where I work. Started as a talk over beer, finished with a bet for fifty nicker that I wouldn't walk a ton in a week. Started off from Glasgow a bloody lifetime ago. Got to a place called Inveraray, four, five days back. Bloke gave me a lift in his car. Commercial, he was; women's dresses. He was making for Fort William, and I was aiming at Inverness, which was where I was to collect the fifty. He'd got a map. I don't have one now; did when I started, not a good one, though; used it for lighting a fire night before last. This bloke went out of his way to give me a lift to Kinloch Rannock, which he said was a fair place to spend the night. Only the road was out, all broken up, and he had to turn and go back. But first he showed me a footpath marked on his map, which would take me to Kirkmalcolm where I could hit the main road again. Which it did—"

"I've seen the place," Maskell broke in quickly to save a time-wasting description.

"Talk about a bloody graveyard." Fairfield shuddered graphically. "Late when I got there. Couldn't believe my eyes, you know? Reckon I must've gone in damn near every house looking for someone, anyone. Dossed down on the floor of one of the shops. Next morning, this morning, didn't much like the look of the road, thought it best if I went back the way I'd come and get another lift. But I couldn't find the bleeding path. Nearly ended up in some sort of bog. So had to come this way after all. Cut myself a stick the first tree I came to for trying out the ground—" He demonstrated with an invisible pole. "Bloody marshes everywhere. Bugger that for a lark. Kettle?" He found it, filled it, set it on the fire, and then consulted his watch after an elaborate wrist manoeuvre. "Hell, is that the hour? I'll have to be on the move again as soon as I've had a drink. Got to get back to Leeds before Thursday or that's my lot. That's when I have to clock back in. My firm's not the easiest mob to work for. Turf me out soon as look—bastards."

Maskell, spooning coffee powder into the cups, tried to hide his disappointment at his not very bright visitor's inability to be of any use at all. Musing, it struck him as being a little odd that here was another man in almost the same unusual position as himself: isolated, lost, and anxious to get back to civilisation. A coincidence?

"Who do you work for?" he asked.

"Nettlefield's," Fairfield told him unenthusiastically, not bothering to look round.

A new name to Maskell, who knew by heart the names of every firm in Saturn.

"The man who gave you the lift—" he started, and then broke off abruptly as the voices began again.

Fairfield, busy balancing the kettle with strategically placed lumps of coal, looked round, enquiringly, asking: "What about him?"

Maskell went to stand by the door. The voices sounded louder, clearer than before. He looked back at the man bending over the grate. It was impossible for Fairfield not to hear them. And yet he was behaving as if there was nothing unusual, nothing worth commenting on, straightening, dusting his hands together, looking up and then, seeing Maskell's expression, raising puzzled dark eyebrows.

"Something wrong?" he wondered.

The voices filled the world. He *must* hear them.

"Did you hear something?" Maskell asked, finding it an effort to keep his voice steady.

"Hear what?" Fairfield listened. "Someone at the front door?" he suggested, and then pulled a face. "Not bloody likely, unless it's that dishwashing fairy of yours. Floorboards creaking, more like."

The voices died away.

"What's that you were saying about the bloke that gave me a lift?" Fairfield asked.

Maskell found his voice. "Nothing." He clenched his fists tightly to stop his hands trembling.

The kettle hissed and spluttered.

"Polly's boiling," Fairfield said cheerfully. Bringing it to the table, he eyed Maskell curiously. "I reckon you must be like me, more used to towns than this sort of thing. Twelve hours of this deathly silence is enough to get on anyone's wick. I can tell you, last night in that bleeding dead village, I could have imagined most anything."

He filled the two cups, took the kettle back to the grate, set it down, then paused with hands on hips, head on one side, to regard once again the shelves of carefully disarranged cups and saucers and plates. "Kinky," he said. "Real kinky." And looked back over his shoulder. "And you say you neither heard nor saw him at it?"

Maskell was recovering from the shock of discovering that the voices hadn't seemingly been heard by his visitor. "I heard something," he said steadily enough. "I was working in one of the other rooms. I thought the sound came from outside."

The other turned from the fascination of the shelves. "Working?"

"Figures, reports. Paperwork."

"Very tasty." Fairfield dragged a chair to the table and sat down. "You in business, then?"

"Saturn," Maskell told him, watching his face.

Fairfield knew the name and made no attempt to disguise the fact. "That mob. Big stuff." Sipping his coffee his eyes returned once more to the shelves, seemingly magnetised by their unusual display. "And that's all he does?" he marvelled. "Just washes dishes?"

"And repacks my suitcases and carts them down to the hall. That was yesterday. I thought it was his way of letting me know I wasn't welcome."

"Kinky," Fairfield said again, picked up his cup and looked very hard at its murky brown contents. "If I was you," he said soberly, not looking up, "I'd take myself away from here. You know. Pretty sharpish-like. It's not your scene. Not mine neither, come to that."

Maskell knew what he was hinting at. Earlier vague suspicions hardened. It was quite possible, after all, that Fairfield was part of what was going on here, his arrival not accidental, one reason for his being here that of indirectly persuading his victim that he was hearing voices that didn't exist. It wouldn't have taken much of an actor to behave as if he had heard nothing. But he had expressed his intention of moving on as soon as he had had a drink. Maskell eyed the bent head of dark tousled hair. And no doubt the victim was supposed to implore him to change his mind and stay. Or else insist upon leaving with him.

Fairfield drained his cup. "I've tasted better, but I'm not

complaining." He grinned with a great show of very large white teeth. "I suppose we leave the dirty cups for the fairies to see to." He pulled back his pullover sleeve to uncover a cheap-looking white-metal watch. "Half eleven. So it's me for the open road and the merry, merry gyppos-o." He came to his feet. "What about you, Maskell? Didn't you say you were thinking of hitting the road this morning?"

"A little later," Maskell said evenly. "Some work to finish first."

Oddly enough, the other made no effort to make him change his mind. And surely any ordinary man, faced with a long walk and knowing someone else was going his way, would have tried to get company for that walk?

In the hall, Maskell held the macintosh-covered bundle while the other slipped his arms through the straps. The heavy pack sat awkwardly on the grey woolen shoulders. Fairfield offered his hand. "Be seeing you, then. Thanks for the coffee." Collecting his homemade pole, he waited for Maskell to open the front door for him.

On the step he regarded the lonely outlook with lacklustre eyes. "Christ. At least it's not raining. That'd have been the last bloody straw." He plodded away down the drive with an exaggerated stoop and bowlegged gait, straightened when he reached the road, put up his hand and was away. Maskell waited until the corner of the house hid him from sight, then went back indoors.

A little way along the rutted, crumbling road, Fairfield stopped and turned. Standing there against the empty sky, pack on back, staff in hand, he had much of the appearance of an old-time pilgrim.

"So what the devil's going on in there?" he asked wonderingly aloud, looking at the house.

⊟⊟ FIVE ⊟⊟

Almost quarter to twelve, getting near to the deadline he had earlier set himself, the morning virtually wasted, thanks to Fairfield, little work done, nothing achieved. Standing in the lounge by his coffee-table desk, Maskell wondered what would now be the most sensible thing to do—stick with his original idea of giving up work at midday to leave in order to find a phone and report his suspicions of Agnew, or carry on working until such times as he had unearthed the proof that must be there, and then set out to look for the telephone.

It seemed to him that his original idea had the edge, for once he had overcome the hurdle of persuading the rest of the board there were good reasons for being suspicious of Agnew, the process of finding the proof would be speeded up.

The decision taken, he piled the papers together, packed them back into the briefcases and took them with him to the kitchen, where the cups and saucers were still on the table, still dirty. He piled them in the sink and opened one of the cupboards to choose cans for his last meal in the house. From the corner of his eye he caught a flicker of movement outside the window. Turning quickly, he was just in time to glimpse what was certainly a man's head and shoulders, going in the direction of either the road or the drive.

Maskell turned and half ran into the hall, flung the front door open and ran along the drive towards the road. His instinctive guess that the man would be making a beeline for the village turned out to be right. They came virtually face to face at the corner of the house, would have collided but both came to a halt in time, the stranger stumbling clumsily back a few paces to crouch, clearly ready to turn and be off in the opposite direction.

At first glance to Maskell, breathing heavily after only that short sprint, a very ordinary, thin-faced individual of indeterminate age, with narrow rounded shoulders and a mass of curly light-brown hair. His eyes were wide and blue, along with the heavy cupid's bow of his thick upper lip giving him an almost babylike appearance.

But then came the second-look impression that there was something about him that wasn't as it should be; an impression of some kind of abnormality suggested by his sleekly smooth, wax-white flesh, the emptiness of the eyes, his partly open mouth. A mental deficiency of some kind, Maskell interpreted; not enough to make him the unkind village idiot of his earlier guess, but not all that far removed. Clean and neat and tidy, he wore an open-necked white shirt, the fake-faded jeans of the day and open sandals. And there was no doubt in Maskell's mind that he was the washer-up of dishes and the arranger of strange designs.

He smiled, holding up his hands, palms outwards. "It's all right." He spoke gently. "There's nothing to be afraid of."

The other straightened, still wary. But while there was no obvious sign of fear in his eyes, when Maskell tried to lessen the distance between them, he moved backwards to maintain it.

"I won't bite you," Maskell said, talking to a child. "What's your name?"

"Brian," the young man said in a soft voice with a rising inflection.

Maskell tried not to sound too knowing. "And I think you're the one who comes and washes up my cups and saucers."

"I've been ill," Brian said, divulging a great secret.

"I am sorry. What was the matter with you?"

"That's why I mustn't come near to you, in case you catch it off me." Brian nodded gravely in time to each utterance. "Anybody could catch it. I'm not supposed to go out."

"Where do you come from, Brian?"

"I was ill, then I got better, and now I'm well, but I mustn't go out and talk to anyone in case I give it to them." It seemed that that was a precaution that had been impressed upon him so deeply as to leave room in his mind for little else.

Maskell tried again. "Where do you live, Brian?"

And this time was successful. The young man stood on tiptoe

to first look over Maskell's shoulder in the direction of the village, then point. "Over there."

A youth who has been ill—mental trouble of some kind?—certainly wouldn't be living alone, least of all in a deserted village. There would be parents; a nurse, perhaps; with luck, a telephone.

"Who do you live with, Brian?" Maskell asked eagerly.

"What's your name?" Brian wanted to know.

Maskell kept a hold on his patience. "Boyd. Do you live with your parents, Brian?"

"Boyd. That's a funny name." But there was no smile for its funniness. Brian never seemed to smile at all; his expression never altered. "I've been ill," he said again, and looked back over his shoulder. "I mustn't talk to no one. I got to go."

He swung clumsily on his heel and was running all in the same movement, arms flapping gawkily, legs loose and ungainly, a queer, half-stumbling gait but one that still managed to cover ground quickly. Maskell took a few instinctive steps forward then stopped, hands on hips, to watch him swerve round the corner of the house, presumably on his way along the terrace and then back up the other side. That's if he was heading for home, as seemed most likely.

Maskell walked quickly along the front of the house with the intention of intercepting him at the other corner, determined not to miss the opportunity of finding out just who was living in the village, and where. But it seemed Brian had more sense than he had given him credit for. When he reached the far corner there was no sign of his quarry. Brian must have carried straight on behind the two outhouses—Maskell, this his first time at this side of the houses, hadn't known of the existence of any outbuildings until now—to work his way home perhaps by a footpath.

Maskell waited a few minutes to be sure, then took a few more minutes to explore the outhouses. The larger one, probably a row of stables at one time, was empty now, but had been used as a garage. There was oil, ancient oil, on the packed-earth floor. By the width and depth of treadmarks, the place had housed three fairly large and heavy vehicles. The smaller building, little more than a shed, was also empty. And although much too small to hold any average-size car, still carried on its earth floor the oil and tire-marks of some vehicle or other. It was the twin lengths of cable hanging from the sloping roof and the large fuse box on the wall that suggested the vehicle had probably been a mobile generator.

Back in the house, about to enter the kitchen, Maskell paused, nose in air, sniffing. Flowers, he thought at first. Carnations. But too cloying, too artificial for that. Scent, then. Faint, but unmistakable, a woman's perfume. Not in the kitchen, but on the threshold between kitchen and hall. It was noticeable at the foot of the stairs; not nearly so strong, but still present, in the lounge where he had spent the night. There were traces of it in the room beyond, as if the wearer—a sudden mental image of gleaming white shoulders, glistening bodice, black-nylon legs—as if its wearer had entered through the french windows there, had made her way as far as the kitchen door, then retraced her steps to leave the same way she had come. Pure conjecture, all that. And the figure conjured up, pure imagination. But the scent in his nostrils was for real. Someone, and it had to be a woman, had been in the house while he was out talking to Brian. Taking advantage of his absence to look for something?

Back in the kitchen—at least, by the absence of scent, she hadn't actually been in here—he hurriedly opened the briefcases. So far as he could tell, everything was intact, nothing had been touched. The most important thing, the sheet of pencilled calculations, was tucked away at the back. He took it out, folded it, made to put it in his inside pocket, remembered he wasn't wearing a jacket, so put it instead in the hip pocket of his trousers.

The voices started up again as he was opening cans, not abruptly as they had the other times, but very quietly at first, a thin whisper, then gradually growing louder until their clamour filled the world. He stood at the kitchen door to listen.

The voices that Fairfield hadn't heard, had pretended not to hear, died away. Maskell finished opening cans with hands that were a little unsteady. He tipped their contents into a saucepan: vegetables, beans, some kind of meat stew. Warming up on the restirred fire it smelt reasonably good. Something to put inside him to keep him going over the God knows how many miles he would have to trudge to the nearest telephone. He toyed with the idea of trying the village again, now he knew for certain that people were living there. But he had looked the place over pretty thoroughly last night and found nothing. It was unlikely he would achieve more if he were to waste time going back again now. It almost seemed as if the people there had gone to some pains to keep their home secret. Ashamed of Brian, perhaps.

He ate the meal standing up, leaning against the open back door, looking out over the remains of the rear terrace and the patch of rough grass where the helicopter had touched down a lifetime ago, across the miles of moorland and marsh and ling to the faraway frieze of blue mountains. He could trace the road along which he would soon be walking. Narrow, deeply rutted; churned-up, almost, it lay like a crumpled length of grey silk between clumps of gorse and clusters of low bushes.

He had prepared too much food. What he couldn't eat he left on the plate. He filled the kettle and set it on the fire. For dessert, he opened a packet of biscuits at random. No longer crisp, and tasting of some artificial sweetener, he tossed them aside. Waiting for the kettle to boil, to make coffee, he had the sudden feeling of not being alone, of there being someone there just behind him. Instead of swinging sharply round, his first instinctive reaction, he forced himself to turn round slowly and casually, half expecting to find Brian there. But the doorway was empty, and there was nobody outside, although there were any number of places, behind bushes and the low terrace walls, where a watcher could be hidden. The damned place was beginning to get through to him. As he had been advised, the sooner he got out of it, the better. He would like to think that Fairfield had been genuine and not, as seemed pretty obvious, part of the conspiracy to unnerve him.

The kettle boiled and he made the coffee. The last drink before setting off. All he would take were the two briefcases; they would be cumbersome enough without anything else. His other things could stay upstairs for the time being. And if Brian wanted to help himself to anything, he was more than welcome.

As he reached for milk to cool the coffee, someone knocked at the front door. No polite tapping, but loud and urgent the thunder that might be made by the hammering of the side of a clenched fist.

This time Maskell allowed himself to react instinctively, putting down the can of milk so quickly its contents fountained up, then hurrying, half running, to throw open the heavy front door. There was no one there. But there *had* been. Whatever else about the damned house might only have been imagination, that dead-rousing knocking had been real. Not Brian; not the type, and he hadn't looked to have the strength to produce such a deafening racket. Face grim, the anger boiling up inside him, Maskell stepped out into the drive, narrowed eyes taking in everything, finding nothing. He ran to the corner of the house where he had met Brian. Then back again, past the front door and along to the outhouses, looking inside each, running round their backs to see if anyone was hiding there. He pushed his way roughly through the small copse of trees whose midnight shadows had once swallowed up a man in a black cloak and a woman in black nylon.

Defeated, baffled, but the anger beginning to pass, he walked slowly back. And in the kitchen, through the spice-aroma of coffee, he was able to detect the smell of the same perfume as before, so cloying as to suggest the greasepaint and powder perfume of a theatre dressing room.

Someone had knocked to draw him away from the kitchen, while someone else, a woman, had taken the opportunity of slipping in to—to do what? Nothing appeared to have been touched. The briefcases were in precisely the same position in which he had left them, propped against the back of one of the chairs. And in any event, at the most he had only been away two or three minutes. Not long enough for anything to have been tampered with. So nothing more than just another move in Agnew's so far pointless war of nerves. No doubt, Maskell thought wryly, time would reveal all. But if they thought he was going to stay on and fight it out, they had another think coming. And if his getting out of the place was playing into their hands, they were welcome, and the best of British luck. He drank his coffee, drained the cup, collected the briefcases and went upstairs with them to get his jacket.

Twenty past twelve by the hall clock, still untampered with. He had thought it later than that, deciding, not liking the idea of strange hands pawing his things, to spare ten minutes or so in repacking his suitcases, ready for them to be collected at some later date. When that would be, he didn't know, didn't much care.

Coming back along the gallery passage with his razor and other things from the bathroom, he fancied he heard a sound from downstairs. The closing of a door, it could have been, and he paused a few seconds at the top of the staircase, leaning over the rail, listening. When the house stayed quiet, he continued on his way back to the bedroom.

The red leather of his suitcase, as he finished packing, and closed it, seemed to be brighter than he remembered; almost shining, as if only recently varnished. And his initials on it, picked out in gold, stood out with startling clarity, with an almost three-dimensional effect. A phenomenon that had to have something to do with the unusually clear air out here, making colours seem brighter, even perhaps tending to heighten the senses. That of touch, certainly, for when he came to grasp the handle, the leather had a new feel to it, the grain seeming to stand out so that his fingers were able to feel a pattern that wasn't there. And when he came to lift the case, to swing it to the floor, it came up like a feather, so light it was, no weight at all; so much so that he laid it flat again and opened it to make sure it was indeed packed full.

His other case, standing at the foot of the bed, that too, now he came to look, had the same appearance of newness, the green leather gleaming as if tooled only yesterday. But unlike its companion, when he came to lift it onto the bed it was so heavy he had to use both hands, then had a struggle to force the lid open.

On top of the shirts he hadn't bothered to unpack was a plain yellow tie.

Not *his* tie . . . He stared down at it. Yellow was a colour he detested. He wondered how it had come to find its way into his case. Then suddenly he realised that this couldn't be his case. Both of his were red, parts of a matching set. Not green, as this one here was. He closed the lid. His own initials leaped up at him from the dark-red leather. Red . . .

He was conscious of a feeling of tightness inside his head, allied with a slight dizziness, not altogether unpleasant. In fact, almost the reverse: the drifting sense of idle well-being, of partial intoxication. Tiredness: that was his trouble. The inevitable outcome of hours of hard graft followed by only half a night's sleep, disturbed sleep at that. Not the best of shapes to be in for the long walk ahead.

He pulled himself together with an effort; what was he doing, wasting time standing here inspecting his suitcases as if he had never seen them before? And inspecting them so closely he was confusing colours. A yellow tie . . . He opened the case again, knowing that there lying on top was the plain blue tie he had bought in Oxford Street to match his blue-striped shirt. Maskell closed the lid again, snapped the lock shut, swung the case effortlessly to the floor.

There was someone, or something, under the bed. The deep fringe of the white counterpane, almost touching the bare boards of the floor, was moving, undulating in a kind of caterpillar motion, as if someone had taken hold of one end of it and was gently and persistently swinging it to and fro.

A cat, perhaps; a stray, found its way in from the moors. Dropping to one knee he reached to lift the counterpane up to look underneath. His fingers seemed to go through it, feeling nothing. He blinked, trying to focus his eyes, tried again. And again his fingers misjudged the distance and closed on nothing. The feeling of dizziness increased. He closed his eyes for a moment, trying to clear his head. When he opened them again it was to find the bed had moved away from him. He started to shuffle forwards on his knees, and the bed adjusted itself, returning to its original position. He used it to push himself back up on his feet.

And now the window was moving, the frame undulating in the same manner as the counterpane, but much more pronounced, so visually disturbing that it induced a feeling of nausea. And now there were sounds . . . a rustling, quite loud, that he was unable to identify until he found the connection between its ebb and flow, and the rise and fall of his own chest to his own breathing.

The window, alive now, came growing from out of its containing wall, reaching out into the room, widening as it came, inexplicably bringing not light with it, but darkness. Darkness that came flooding in from all sides, reaching out to encircle him like the scimitar flanks of an attacking army.

Shapes moved ghostlike across an arena of which he was the centre, twisting, turning, gyrating, now huge and monstrous, now shrinking almost to nothing. Light came greyly. A new shadow came growing up from out of the grey emptiness, spreading tall and wide, becoming a man wearing a long black cloak, his feet in the depths, his bare head, with its peculiar plastered curls, towering to touch the sky.

Arms outflung, cloak sweeping, the shape spun towards him, enveloped him, passed by. And behind came the scent of perfume and curves and smoothness and silkiness and long-nylon legs and rounded thighs and swelling breasts that rose from the black frills of a scarlet bodice. Warm sweet breath on his face, and soft delicacy touching, tantalising and drifting lightly across his forehead and cheeks. And warm sweet breath on his mouth, and the rich softness of lips in a moment's touch that lasted an eternity, and then the warmth and softness were snatched away and the blackness was sweeping him along a tunnel towards a distant speck of light. And then that last faint far-off glimmer faded, and he was alone in a night which had no sunset, no dawn, which went on forever and forever . . .

Fairfield, hiker's pack on back, pilgrim staff in hand, trudged wearily up the drive from road to front door, limping a little from where he had stubbed his foot against one of the stones of the road's broken surface. He used his staff to rap on the front door. When there was no reply, he banged it against the panels, impatiently, growling under his breath. He had not met Maskell along the road, and so he should still be in the house, for all he had said he would be leaving. Fairfield was far from happy about being back here again, wishing very much he hadn't had to return, but feeling he had no alternative. He was also tired and thirsty. He banged again. "Come on, for God's sake. I know you must be in there." Unless, and he turned to look in the direction of the village, the poor bastard hadn't believed that bit about the road that way being out, kaput, finito. If he hadn't, and that was what he was trying, then he'd soon be back.

Fairfield limped round the side of the house. The back door opened at the mere lifting of the latch. He called: "Ahoy there, Maskell!" while he wriggled his arms out of the straps and let his pack fall to the floor. In the hall he rapped his staff on the stone flags and shouted again: "You upstairs, Maskell?"

No reply, and so it looked like he had gone off to the village. He climbed the stairs one step at a time, trailing the staff, rattling along the rails. He dropped it at the top of the stairs when he went into one of the bathrooms. Emerging again, instead of going back down the stairs he carried on across the gallery, looking for the bedroom Maskell had been using, wondering if he had left anything behind.

He found the room. "Christ . . ." he breathed fearfully from the doorway.

Maskell lay sprawled at an angle across the bed, dangling head almost touching the floor, his eyes closed, not seeming to be breathing.

SIX

Fairfield had been downstairs to make some tea. "Lousy, but it's better than the muck you call coffee. Best we can manage, I'm afraid. A drop of short would have done you a bloody sight more good." He set the teapot, two cups, can of milk and bag of sugar down on the dressing table. "Do me more good, too," he added wryly. "Just for a minute, I made sure you'd bought it. Heart attack; something like that. I damn near had one myself." He slopped tea into the cups, handed one to Maskell. "And how d'you feel now, old son?" His concern sounded genuine enough.

"Fine." Maskell sipped the tea. It tasted better than it looked.

"Good." The other eyed him closely. "It sounds like you had yourself quite a ball after I left. I wasn't all that long away, either." He looked at his watch. "Only one now."

Maskell put his cup down. "And you say the road's out in the other direction as well." Not a question; a resigned statement.

"Barely a mile of it." Fairfield, ignoring his tea, folded his grey woolen arms. "Couldn't be much more. There's a signpost. What the hell did it say? 'Ballachulish. Forty-five miles.' Christ, I thought; nothing nearer? There must be, I thought. So on I went. Round the corner, and nothing. Road just like a string of bombs had dropped along it. Just rubble. I went a bit along it, then that gave out too. Nothing after that. I didn't fancy sinking up to my neck in one of the bogs, so I turned round and came back. No wonder there's no traffic, I thought. Bleeding road has no beginning and no end. So I don't know how that loony type, Brian, or whatever you call him, got here. Maybe he flew; like you." He paused. "Finding you all flaked out—that was bloody real anyway." He unfolded his arms. "Be right back," he said from the doorway.

Downstairs, he went quickly through all the rooms, looking carefully about him, lifting his head from time to time to sniff the air. He opened the front door and walked along the drive to the corner where Maskell had met Brian. After a while he came back indoors again, took another look inside the kitchen, another sniff at the air, then went back upstairs to where Maskell, a lock of dark-bronze hair falling over a palish forehead, was still on the bed, propped up against the wall, busy examining the contents of the two briefcases.

"All right so far as I can tell," he told Fairfield's slanted enquiring brows. The all-important sheet of paper was still in his hip pocket; that was the first thing he had checked.

Fairfield picked up his cup. "No signs of anything anywhere downstairs. No smells or anything. Went outside. Patch of softish ground where you said you met the loony. Nothing on it, though. No footprints." He sipped the tea. "He could have been standing on the gravel, though."

Maskell stared up at him across the tops of the briefcases.

"You think none of it happened," he remarked equably. "I imagined it all."

"You don't sound like you'd mind if I said I did."

Maskell swung the briefcases, one at a time, to the floor. He was beginning to get tired of trundling them around, continually having to open and close them.

"I know how it all must sound," he said.

"The loony type. Him I'd buy, at a pinch. But not the gent in the Dracula get-up and the bint in the Soho fancy dress. I mean, fair play and all that."

"Brian was real enough," Maskell said. "And the hammering at the door. And the smell of perfume."

"And your cases changing colour, and the window coming out of its frame to hit you?"

"I don't know," Maskell said.

"Dope. You know. Drugs. I got that idea while you were telling me all about it. Somebody fixed you. But your eyes don't show any signs, your pupils look normal enough to me, there's no trace of anything in the cup you must have drunk your coffee from, no smell that I could pick up, and you say you don't feel any kind of aftereffect?"

"I feel fine," Maskell said truthfully.

"I don't get it." The other refilled his cup, offered the teapot. "You?"

"No, thanks," Maskell said, and the telephone started ringing.

"Last night," Fairfield said in the overkeen manner of one trying to be helpful, "you say you think some sound or other woke you up. What kind of sound?"

The ringing seemed to be everywhere, so loud the instrument might have been there in the room between them.

"What kind of sound would you say?" Fairfield asked again.

"You're not deaf," Maskell said, fighting the urge to shout. "You must hear it. Just as you must have heard the voices before. You're only pretending not to, and that has to be because somebody's paying you to try to make me believe I'm going out of my mind. And I'm pretty sure I know who's paying you. I think I know why."

"Only pretending . . ." Fairfield, confused, stared at him. "Voices? I don't think I'm with you. Are we still talking about last night?"

"Oh, for God's sake—" Maskell started angrily, letting himself go. The ringing broke off abruptly, as it had once before, in mid-pattern. "We're talking about now," he said loudly. "The sound that stopped just a second ago. The telephone. You heard it. For God's sake, man, stop your pretending."

"Yes—" Fairfield scratched one side of his head, disarranging still further his already disordered black hair. "The telephone. I didn't think there was—" He broke off. "Oh, hell. I said it before, Maskell. For your own sake, you ought to get away from here. Me as well, before I start seeing and hearing things too." His concern seemed a very genuine thing. As was his hastily added: "Not that you've really anything to worry about yet."

"I want to get away from here," Maskell said, voice normal again, "not because I'm at all afraid of losing my mind." At least that was almost the truth. "But because there's a very good reason why I must contact my firm as quickly as possible."

"Fair enough." The other spread his hands. "So what do you suggest, then?"

Maskell knew exactly what the present position was, down to every last detail. Despite all that had happened, there was not the slightest hint of haziness inside his head. It was as if problems requiring answers were being fed from some outside source into the intricacies of his mind, there to be dealt with, by some means beyond his control, with machinelike accuracy and efficiency, the answers being delivered and presented with the black-and-white clarity of print on tape.

Fairfield was part of the conspiracy. Check. Any advice he might give, no matter how apparently well-intentioned, could only be to his detriment, and so must be ignored. Check. Any help he might offer must be similarly treated. Check. Correction. Cancel last instruction. Substitute following: Any help he might offer that fits in with acceptable plan of escape can be accepted with reservations. Check. Time? Twelve and a half minutes before two o'clock. Assuming dusk to be at eight-fifteen, six hours, twenty-seven and a half minutes of practical daylight left. Check. Briefcases too heavy to carry any distance. Find suitable hiding place for that containing the more important papers. Check. Wash. Put on jacket. Start now.

The machine inside his head clicked to a halt. Maskell swung his feet to the ground.

"You have something in mind?" Fairfield wondered.

Maskell spoke with a crisp assurance that was unusual even in one in his position of authority. "Bathroom first. Then I have to find somewhere to hide one of my briefcases. That should take no more than five minutes. Then I intend to walk to the village to find either the footpath by which you arrived, or better still, the place where Brian is living."

"Yes." The other, massaging the tip of his overlong chin, studied Maskell closely from under puzzled brows. "Sounds reasonable enough. Nothing else, anyway, is there?"

He went out into the passage in Maskell's wake to watch him go along the passage. He rubbed the side of his head again. "What's with him now?" He tried an idea that had occurred to him before. "Dope?" But that wasn't it. If there was somebody mucking about, if the loony type and the rest were real after all, and they wanted to fix him with some kind of dope, they'd use something to slow him down, not the sort that would make him snap back like a rubber band. Bringing him all to a head like this was the very last thing they'd want.

Maskell returned from the bathroom, went briskly into his bedroom, emerged with his jacket over one arm, a briefcase in his other hand.

"Take your places for hunt the slipper," Fairfield muttered under his breath, and nodded at the case. "That the one you have to hide?" And when Maskell didn't bother to reply: "Something important?"

Maskell paused at the top of the stairs, his mind assembling facts. Fairfield is being paid to play a role. Check. A mercenary, with no knowledge of what is involved. So the possibility exists that if he were made aware of the true facts, the gravity of the situation, he might panic and renege on his employer, changing from an enemy into an ally. But not all cards to be laid on the table. Check. The ace to remain in his hip pocket.

He asked: "Do you know anything of finance?"

Fairfield, startled, gestured. "Some. You know. The rudiments. I'm more administration."

"If the contents of this case were to fall into the wrong hands," Maskell said with all the impressiveness he could muster, "it could mean the loss to my people of something in the region of ten million sterling."

"Ten million," the other echoed incredulously. "There isn't that much money. And you think that that's what's going on here?" His gesture included the house. "Someone trying to get their hands on whatever you've got in that case?"

Not the reaction Maskell had hoped for. Instead, one of barely disguised disbelief. He tried another line, one much nearer the truth. "It isn't as simple as that. The man behind all this doesn't need to get his hands on these papers. He's already working behind the scenes, and will continue to do so for as long as I am safely out of his way. I'm the only one who can stop him."

"Now I see," Fairfield said in his helpful, understanding voice. "That's why you've been dumped out here in the middle of nowhere. And the loony and the refugees from Hammer Films are all in his pay."

Maskell gave up. He tapped the case. "I'd be obliged if you'd stay up here while I dispose of this."

"Anything you say," the other said agreeably, too agreeably, and seated himself on the top step, large hands resting on grey-clad knees.

Maskell continued on down the stairs, across the hall to the room with the leather chairs, and so finally out to the small out-building that had presumably once housed a generator. His new, efficient mind, seeking a suitable hiding place, had remembered the large wall-attached fuse box, that had all the appearance of having been constructed on the spot, and not installed as a complete unit. The assessment was right. The panel of fuses came forward when he pulled, exposing a cavity behind. He pulled some cables away, tucked others around the sides, until he had made a space large enough to take the briefcase. With the panel replaced and the loose cables disposed of under one of the bushes, there was nothing to show that the fuse box had been tampered with. One thing less to worry about. Hiding the case had just been a regular security measure. He didn't think that Brian or Fairfield or anyone else out here was particularly interested in its contents. They were all here for a very different reason.

He went back into the house to where Fairfield still sat obediently at the top of the stairs with something of the nose-through-the-bannisters look of a small boy peeping down at a grownups' party.

"Mission accomplished," Fairfield murmured under his breath. "All set?" he asked aloud, coming to his feet.

By way of reply, Maskell opened the front door and stepped outside, putting on his jacket as he went.

Fairfield kicked his pack in passing. "I'm not lugging you round any more." But collected his homemade staff. "I'd better take this along."

And outside, hurrying in Maskell's wake, he found himself attracted by the small copse of trees from whose moonlit shapes and shadows Maskell's mind had drawn the couple of weirdos. Awakened suddenly from sound sleep—and Maskell still hadn't answered his question about the sort of sound that woke him—only half and half, bleary-eyed and all the rest, Christ, one could imagine anything. But on the other hand, Fairfield supposed, it was possible there was a family—father, mother and son, all nutters of one kind or another, the son some sort of invalid, pigging it like gyppos in the village. It would be just as well, he told himself, covertly eyeing his companion's profile as they walked together towards the road, if they did turn out to be real.

The sky had clouded over. The light breeze was comfortably warm for all the miles of marsh and moorland it must have travelled to reach them. A wild man's country of spear grass, reeds, bracken and purple thistle. Behind it all, the thin border of distant mountains. Then the straggle of small, unhappy trees that marked the fringe of the village; the first solitary cottage, then rows on either side, lifeless and lost. Dust had settled and hardened in the verges of the stone-flagged pavements. Grey stone showed in patches where whitewash had weathered from cottage walls. There was a birdhouse of stone, for the birds—none here now—that must have left when the people went.

From Fairfield, a growled: "I thought I'd seen the last of this bloody joint."

Maskell's new confidence and strange clarity of mind were beginning to wane. He tried the doors of the cottages, looked into echoing ghost-rooms, trod gardens that had become small oases of weeds in a stone jungle. Watched by Fairfield, he searched for something, anything, that might indicate living people had passed this way recently.

At the triangle of grass that seemed to mark the centre of the village, where four roads met, he paused, suddenly feeling unaccountably tired and lifeless, finding it hard to resist the invitation of the stone-slab bench beneath the drunken signpost.

With the aid of his staff, Fairfield struck a pose. "Lord of all I survey. Did you get that at school too? Now I know how that bloke Selkirk must have felt." He used the staff as a pointer, indicating the road straight ahead. "That's the way I came in yesterday. Forks a way back, just round the bend. Tried both roads to make sure. Like they'd been cut off with a knife. You can go see for yourself if you like." He nodded in turn to those on either side. "These too. That goes to a farm. The other ends up in a patch of black slime." The staff swung like a gigantic compass needle. "The path I came in by must cross the moors about there. I can show you roughly where it hits the road, not the exact spot. If I knew that, I wouldn't be bloody here now."

But for the moment Maskell was more concerned with possible dwellings than escape routes. He felt that if he were faced with the problem of finding somewhere to live without attracting attention, himself and two other people, he would go for a larger building in preference to a cottage. The post office; the pub; even the church. Especially if it had a crypt. And the pub might have a cellar. The church squatted square and grey on the right of the grass triangle. Facing it, on the other side, the faded but still colourfully garish sign of The Highlander still waited with welcoming arms for the ghost parishioners of the past.

The empty arms now of the long empty room with low-raftered ceiling and faded green walls. Dusty inglenook seats guarded an empty fireplace. A circle in pockmarked green showed where a dart board must once have hung. All that remained of the shelves behind the bar and the bar counter itself were scars on the wall and stone floor. No signs of life. No cellar flap. Nothing.

Then something. Maskell, leading the way into one of the smaller rear rooms, stopped, nose in air. Not cheap scent this time, but the strong, unmistakable smell of cooking. Bacon, he identified, sniffing; beans; maybe sausages; certainly coffee. And fresh.

Oddly, Fairfield could smell nothing. "That scent again, is it?" he hazarded, testing the air. "Your nose must be better than mine. I can't pick up a thing. Just musty to me." And, surprised: "Cooking?" He tried again, looking round the tiny room with its prison-cell window. "No. In any case, I wouldn't think anyone would hang out in here. No signs of anything, anyway."

Which was true enough. No grate which might have had tell-tale ashes; no stains on the stone-flagged floor; no scraps of paper. Only a smell that, strong as it was, Fairfield seemed unable to detect. Just as he had been unable to hear the strident ringing of a telephone bell. Without bothering to look in any of the other rooms, Maskell went out into the open again, no patience left at all now for someone who, after this last little episode, must certainly be regarded as part and parcel of Agnew's conspiracy. He walked across the patch of grass to the short stone path that led between banks of coarse grass to the church door.

A door of weather-worn oak and rusty iron studs that creaked dismally open to reveal an interior of depressing emptiness. Plain glass to the narrow windows, no heretic colours. Cold stone floor, cold as charity. Maskell had looked inside once before, and so knew what to expect. But that last time he had done nothing more than shoulder the door open, take in the echoing emptiness and close it quickly again. This time he looked for but failed to find the entrance to a crypt. Why this mental harping on a crypt? Who in God's name would want to live in such a place? A man with a death-mask face and unnatural hair and sweeping black cloak. Dracula, risen with sundown. And one of his hand-maidens. Maskell had to forcibly wrench his mind free of the idiot's path it was travelling, a pendulum reaction, it almost seemed, to its former machinelike efficiency. And succeeding in regaining common sense, a small wave of weariness made him stop and rest his hand against the ice-cold wall, closing his eyes to the greyness around him. Only moments, then it passed and he was himself again, idiocy forgotten, ignoring Fairfield's voiced concern, trying the small door set deep in the stonework.

It led to a flight of narrow and incredibly worn stone steps that spiralled dangerously upwards, leading to the belfry. Leading rather to what once had been the belfry: no bells there now, only the massive beams from which they must have once hung. And here, surprisingly, a kind of projecting ledge had been constructed, not of new wood, but of wood certainly much newer than the rest. And from this hangman's platform new wooden steps led upwards again, up and out into the open, with all round the moorland, and the air alive and the ground a thousand miles below.

As old as the hills themselves, the grey stone of which the square tower had been built. But in places along the top of the low enclosing wall, the ancient stone had been chipped away and patches of still new-looking concrete laid. Set in those unsightly, out-of-place scars were several round metal sockets—dirt had accumulated in them, so some time since they had been used—giving the impression of being designed to take the supports of instruments of some kind.

Pointless to waste time on them, Maskell felt. Even more pointless to ask Fairfield if he knew what they might be for. They had no bearing on his reason for coming up here. From this vantage point, the village laid out like a map all around, it might be possible to spot what he had earlier failed to find from the road: the incoming wires of a telephone.

From the south, they would come; and so it was in that direction that he immediately turned, leaning over the wall, his gaze sweeping slowly across the so very small collection of roofs, finding nothing there, so lifting to move further back, away to the outskirts; and nothing there, no poles, so even further out still, and there the forked roads Fairfield had spoken about—at least that had been the truth—and neither had he been lying when he had said something about their being cut off as by a knife, for that was almost precisely the impression they gave from up here. So, no wires in that direction, and no way out, unless it was possible to find the elusive path, and of that there was no sign to be seen. Maskell turned to look in the opposite direction, back towards the house, moving to join Fairfield, already on that side of the tower, hands resting on the worn stone, his gaze narrowed into the distance.

Over on the right something moved. Just for an instant, black dazzled against green, and then, quite clearly visible, the man in the black cloak—real, not imagination after all—walked across the afternoon moorland, bareheaded as before, the scarlet lining of his cloak showing in startling flashes of colour, his face a white oval of death, broken by the black gashes of eyebrows, eyes and mouth. Gliding, rather than walking, it seemed; his feet barely seeming to touch the ground—if there was marshland there, he was walking over it—coming towards the village at an angle, so close now that soon he would be hidden from view by one of the outlying cottages.

Maskell pointed. "There. Do you see?" Purposely, he kept his voice calm and matter-of-fact.

Fairfield turned his head to look. He narrowed his gaze even more, a sailor on the bridge of a ship, one hand raised to shield his eyes from a sun that wasn't there.

"What am I supposed to be looking for?" he wanted to know, staring straight at the man in the cloak.

"Deaf, with no sense of smell, and now blind into the bargain," Maskell said thinly.

"I should be seeing something out there?" Fairfield leaned dangerously over the low wall, still looking directly at the man with the black cloak, still looking in that direction after he had vanished from sight behind the cottage to leave the landscape empty.

"You missed your vocation," Maskell told him, turning away, making towards the wooden staircase. "You should have gone on the stage." He tried to force niggling doubt from his mind, starting to climb back down, not wasting breath in replying when Fairfield, close behind, asked if it was: "The loony type—Brian, as you call him?"

Maskell, emerging into the open again, became conscious of a feeling of depression that had come settling down on him like a black pall, augmenting the tiredness, dulling his senses. It suddenly required conscious effort to set in motion the machinery of thought. It seemed his mind could cope now with only one idea at a time. He had climbed the tower to look for telegraph poles. No poles, so no phone in the village. No point now trying to track down Brian. Even if he did manage to find where he was living, the odds were the people with him would turn out to be tarred with the same brush as Fairfield, part of the same conspiracy, at the best, not to be relied on.

Frowning, one hand pressed to his forehead, Maskell tried to concentrate. He had come to the village with two things in mind. Telephone, and something else. It came to him as he walked slowly down the stone-flagged path to the dusty road. Fairfield's vanishing footpath. If it had ever existed. But the roads were out—that much he had seen for himself—and there had to be an alternative way into the place, which meant that that part of the story might be true. Of the two roads forking ahead, it must link with that on the left and on its lefthand side. He turned for confirmation. But his companion was not close behind as he had imagined, was nowhere in sight. He called: "Fairfield?" waited, then walked back along the road and up the path. The church was empty; so was the overgrown churchyard; so, for their visible lengths, were all four roads leading from the green.

How he had managed it, Maskell didn't know, for his back had been turned only a few short minutes. But during that time, Fairfield, for reasons of his own, had managed, unobserved, to slip away, vanishing as quickly as if he had never been there at all.

▣▥▣ SEVEN ▥▣▥

The afternoon was all the emptier and silent for Fairfield's going. Alone in the world, Maskell sat on the low stone wall that bordered the small enclosed wilderness of the churchyard. What Fairfield chose to do was entirely his own concern. If he wanted to slip away without saying a word, that was up to him. No use trying to think of a reason for his action; reason had no part in anything that happened in this damn place.

He felt weary and dispirited, incapable almost of thought itself, drained and empty, unable to shake off the cloud of depression. Too oppressive a state in one unaccustomed even to moodiness to be natural. Induced by some means or other, and so it would pass.

It took a conscious effort of strength to push himself to his feet again. He stood for a few moments, collecting himself, then set off along the lefthand fork. The row of by now monotonous white-walled cottages petered out. Moorland greens and browns lapped at the verge of the crumbling road. There were no signs close to of the path that had been invisible from a distance. Slime glistened evilly; there were pools of steel-grey water; a stretch of green brighter than the rest turned out to be the deception of scum on marsh.

Maskell walked the road until there was no road left to walk. If there was a path, it was impossible to find. And without it, there was no hope of escape that way; nobody in their right mind would trust themselves to that treacherous wilderness. Much as he hated the idea he saw nothing for it but to return to the house. Whatever else it had come to stand for, it did at least represent food and shelter and a place to sleep.

He turned to walk back. His mind, he noted with relief, was beginning to clear, the pall of depression to lift. When he reached the green, sight of the church reminded him of the man in the black cloak. In his mind's eye was an aerial picture of the precise cottage behind which that crow-black figure had vanished. Maskell turned to walk along the road that led towards the cottage.

A breeze played momentarily across his face, pleasantly warm and tinged with the faint sweetness of open-air growing things. It touched off a responsive chord in his mind, bringing vividly back a memory that had never been far from the front of his thoughts ever since the dream hallucination.

He reached up to touch his mouth, letting his fingers pass lightly across his lips, trying to match the sensation now with that in the dream. There was a difference—of course there was a great difference—for the touch on his lips now was that of his own hand, and he *knew* it was only that. In the dream the touch had been lighter, softer. And before that silky warm contact —and he was very sure about this—there had been the warm sweetness of breath on his face. And then the touch of lips, that couldn't have been anything else but the soft touch of a woman's lips, on his. The rest might have been hallucination, but that part had been real.

Twin rows of look-alike cottages came to an end. Then came the lone cottage of his mental picture—to check, he turned to look back at the church, testing the angle. Doorless and windowless, it was clearly even less habitable than any other of the places he had explored. He didn't have to go inside, only peer through the gaping window gaps, to know that nobody lived there, that nobody had used it for a very long time. He turned to retrace his steps.

While the depression had lifted and his mind had cleared, the feeling of tiredness had persisted. Only a short walk, less than a mile, but one that taxed his strength. So much so that, turning into the drive, he slipped and fell, and to straighten up again was reduced to ignominiously having to use both hands like an old man.

Despite everything, he was relieved to be back in the house. Fairfield's pack was where he had left it in the hall. To hell with it, to hell with its owner, and to hell with a grate that had to be raked out, relaid with paper and sticks and coal, and relighted, before he could start thinking about making a cup of tea.

But first he went to see if there were any signs of anyone having been in the house during his absence. The dirty dishes were still in the sink, which meant Brian hadn't paid one of his cleaning-up visits. In his bedroom, the two suitcases and briefcase were just as he had left them. Or had they moved a fraction? It seemed to him that when he had earlier left them they had been more spaced out than they were now. Not that it mattered much if they had been interfered with. He went out to the generator shed, and there the same story: briefcase intact behind fuse board, but the feeling that its position had been slightly changed. Its contents, anyway, were intact. Even down to the sheets on which he had tried to break down the code. Not that they would have been of much use to anyone without the information on the sheet now in his hip pocket, but just to be on the safe side he abstracted the several sheets, folded them and added the slim wad to the sheet already in his pocket.

Back in the kitchen he decided it wasn't worth the effort to relight the fire. Instead, he wandered over to the cupboards to see if there was anything drinkable there among the mass of cans and packets he so far hadn't bothered about examining. There was fruit juice. Better still, several cans of lager. He took one of them, along with a clean cup from the idiot's arrangement on the shelf, back to the table.

The lager wasn't too warm to be unpleasant. He emptied the can, collected another from the cupboard. He felt all the better for the drink. The tiredness was still there, but the depression had lifted completely. His mind was alive again; he found himself able to think clearly and rationally again. He tried to think of a reason why Fairfield should have vanished in the way he had. It seemed likely it was simply another piece to add to the background of confusion and unreality that was so painstakingly being built up. So *unnecessarily* being built up, it seemed to Maskell's refound clarity of mind, if the sole purpose of the conspiracy was simply to keep him out of the way while Agnew completed his financial double-dealings.

And so for the first time he found himself with doubts about the origins of his present discomfort. Not the someone above him on the board, as he had been so sure, but why not someone below? The overambitious junior, waiting to step into the shoes of his superior, removed from his position because of the unhinged state of his mind. A great deal of trouble and expense involved, but worth every penny when the prize is big enough. As it certainly would be in his case. That sort of thing had been worked before; it would be tried again. Sipping his lager, eyes narrowed thoughtfully, Maskell ran through the list of possibles in his own specific field. Offhand, he could think of three who wouldn't hedge at such a scheme, particularly if they had the backing of a higher-up, as one of them had. Dog eat dog. It was an idea worth considering as an alternative to his original notion. The causation of mental confusion . . . enough to convince an expert that here was a man who, through overwork and strain, could no longer be regarded as fit for office. An expert . . . Sir John Mellish-Rae, it would be in his case. One of the Gods come down from Olympus. A man who was no fool and would take a very great deal of convincing before passing the death sentence on one of Conrad Earlam's personally selected bright young men. And what chance had this scheme now of succeeding?

It was getting through to him. Constant dripping will wear away the hardest stone. Maskell, staring down at the tabletop, asked himself why it was when he had seen the man with the black cloak he hadn't rushed out of the church to try to intercept him. It could have been because just at that time he was feeling unusually weary and dispirited. On the other hand, it was possible that subconsciously he had accepted the weird shape gliding over the marshy land as being nothing more than a hallucination. Accepted it . . . accepted the fact he was seeing and hearing things that weren't there. The makings of insanity. A cold emptiness grew in his stomach.

"Hello," Brian's quiet child's voice said from behind him.

Maskell swung round so violently he knocked his cup over, its contents frothing brownly across the white tabletop. Brian stood unsmilingly in the hall doorway, still wearing the white shirt, blue

jeans and sandals that had something of the appearance of a
special kind of school uniform.

"Where the devil—" Maskell started in a voice made harsh by
startlement, then broke off, taking a deep breath, collecting himself, starting again. "How did you get in the house, Brian?"

"You've upset your drink," the other said with some concern,
the first sign of any emotion he had so far displayed. And, as if
repeating a lesson learned: "If it isn't wiped up soon it will leave
a mark." He made no move to tackle the cleaning himself.

"Right." Maskell went to the sink, came back with the dishcloth, wiped the table, tossed the rag back into the sink and then
refilled his cup. As an afterthought, he held up the can. "Do you
want a drink?"

"I come to see if you've been ill," Brian said, again with concern.

His childlike innocence called for honesty. "I haven't been very
well, certainly," Maskell told him, the events of the past few
hours in mind: the hallucinations, the strange clarity of mind
followed by the unnatural tiredness and the terrible depression.
And then, struck by a sudden thought: "What made you think I
might have been ill?"

Brian shuffled his sandalled feet on the stone flags. "It was me
that did it."

"You?" Was it actually possible that this halfwit youth had
been responsible for at least some of the things that had been
happening? Drugs . . . Fairfield had suggested dope. It could
have been something like that. "You mean you gave me something—" But putting it that way might be too complicated for
the halfwit to understand. It would have to be worded as simply
as possible. "You did something to me to make me sick?"

"I didn't mean to. They said I would, but I tried not to. I
came back to see."

Who "they" were could wait. "You gave me something." Maskell remembered the coffee, the last thing he had taken before
the hallucinations started. "You put something in my coffee."

But that wasn't it. It took Brian a few moments to absorb the
suggestion, then: "Oh, no!" He was shocked by the very idea.

"Oh, I didn't do that. It was because—well, I told you—because I'd been ill too."

So back with the infectious, contagious thing again. Disappointed, Maskell tried something else. "Who was it who told you not to—"

The telephone started ringing. Brian's pale waxen head jerked round in the direction of the sound. "What's that bell ringing?" He went into the hall.

And then the significance of it broke on Maskell. Relief surged, expanded, exploded. "You mean you can hear it?" He followed into the hall. "You can really hear it?" The relief that somebody else apart from himself could actually hear the sound was an almost physical thing.

Brian was looking up the stairs. "Is it up there? What is it—is it a telephone? I didn't know there was a telephone in this house."

Filled with the new emotion, Maskell went to stand at the foot of the stairs. The sound did seem to be coming from somewhere above. But then he had noticed that before. It was good to have even that one small thing confirmed. But what was most important of all, more important than finding the instrument itself, was the knowledge that the sound was real after all, not a hallucination, but real . . . And then came another thought, chilling, frightening, swamping the sense of relief.

The ringing died away.

It was possible that Brian had only heard the sound because, like it, he was a hallucination himself. Not real, neither sound nor person. But he *was* real; he was flesh and blood. The sound had stopped, but Maskell still stared up the stairs, afraid to turn round. If he did turn, Brian would be standing there, real, alive. He had only to reach out to touch him to prove that. Touch him . . .

Maskell turned round. The hall was empty. He half ran into the kitchen, that also empty, but the back door standing open a fraction. He couldn't remember if it had been open before. Pushing it wide, he stepped outside. There was no sign of Brian. But he knew from the other time how quickly he could vanish when he wanted to. By now, ungainly limbs flying, he could be halfway home. He was solid and real—he had to be—and so was everything else. And Fairfield, an actor, perhaps, had been playing the part he had been paid to play.

Maskell came back into the kitchen, closing the door on a sky that had lowered and a breeze that had become appreciably cooler. But a long way off evening yet: only a few minutes after four. Standing by the table, his thin hands resting on its white wood top, he looked out of the window at the leaden sky.

His one thought now was to get away from this place while he was still capable of rational thought and behaviour. Half of him knew that what had been happening was reality made to appear unreal and impossible. But the other part was already beginning to accept that he had been experiencing hallucinations. There was no way of telling just how much more his divided self could take.

His mouth had become dry; there was some difficulty in swallowing. He drained the cup, opened another can of lager, refilled the cup and took it over to the window.

The road out there, pointing to the north, led nowhere, Fairfield had said, petering out into impassable rubble. There it lay, inviting him to try for himself, nothing to prevent him so doing. Which meant that for at least once Fairfield had been speaking the truth. Neither had he lied about the state of the roads and the impossible-to-find footpath that led south from the deserted village. On the face of it, the place was virtually cut off. But there were other people here—two at least. They could have come, like himself, by helicopter. But that possibility seemed so remote as not to be worth considering.

Maskell pressed one hand to where the skin of his forehead seemed suddenly to have become dry and taut. He had tried all this before, this logical assembling of facts. It might work in the city, behind a desk, with a column of figures to analyse. But there seemed no place for rational thought in this world of empty skies and moorland.

One of the taps was dripping. He hadn't noticed it before, but now he found himself studying the shape and symmetry of the globule as it formed, shining and pulsating; he found himself waiting, poised, for it to plummet down to the yellow stone of the sink. He found himself cringing at the sound it made, a sound that seemed to burst inside his head.

He put his cup down hastily so that he could use both hands to turn off the tap as far as it would go. He was just in time to prevent the next globule from falling. He reasoned vaguely that the oddly penetrating sound must have had something to do with the echo quality of the deep sink. Of the deep, bright-yellow sink: a glowing, burning yellow that dazzled so fiercely he was forced to narrow his eyes against it. His narrowed lids created the optical illusion of patches of blue forming on the yellow, like oil on water, collecting in the corners and climbing the sides, spreading until the whole of the sink was bathed in iridescent blue.

So intense were the colours that the air above seemed to quiver, the ground shuddering in sympathy. Maskell closed his eyes. When he opened them again the sink had returned to its normal colour. He turned round. The room seemed much longer than before, the table farther away than he had thought, and distorted in some odd fashion, so that the side farthest away seemed closer to him than the nearest side, a disquieting displacement of perspective that made everything out of focus. He had to close his eyes again, this time against a small wave of vertigo. When he cautiously opened them, the table had resumed its proper shape and position.

There was a strong smell in the room: rich, heavy, suggestive of fermentation. It came, he discovered, from the empty cup on the window ledge behind him, and from the empty lager cans on the table. When he came to pick up the cans, to drop them in the cardboard rubbish box in the corner, his hands seemed to go right through them. He experienced the same difficulty in judging distances that he had once before when trying to touch the coverlet on his bed. The notion that what was happening to him now was the same thing that had happened earlier was there, in his thoughts, but too elusive for him to grasp and examine and compare. His mind had become incapable of encompassing more than one idea at a time. It had found and dealt with the tap, the sink, the lager, and now the cans. And now the drum . . .

The slow, steady beat of a gigantic drum, growing from nothing to fill the house like—like the pulse of the house; like the house was a living thing, and this steady hollow beat its heart. In the hall was the heart, coming from the old grandfather clock and its slow, steady ticking. A heart, and the house coming warm and alive all around him. The staircase, sweeping off and up into the mists of infinity; the doors, surging ever upwards, straining to break from the containing walls; the walls themselves, pulsating in time to the beat of the heart, pressing in on him from all sides, swooping away again in the movments of some maniac rounddance. And the house, alive, enfolding him, talking to him . . . not in words, but in thoughts and images and memories and faraway voices. The voices of the men who had once lived in the house, had worked here, fighting to save others and themselves from the sickness, their only link with the outside world the telephone. A sickness without a name, brought to the lonely village by the man who wore the black cloak: an evil being; a dead man, risen from the grave and walking; the walking dead. And with him, another of his kind, a woman, both carriers of the deadly virus, both battening on the death it brought. Walking the roads—Maskell could see them, the man with billowing cloak, the woman with evil silken limbs. Driving the people away; the village deserted. Only a handful left: the braver ones, those who stayed to fight; and those not capable of understanding, the mindless ones. And those, for some reason, were able to take the sickness and survive it, but becoming carriers themselves. And Brian was one of those. But the others, the few who knew what they were doing, what the risk was; they took refuge in the house, and from there fought the plague and its carriers, until they could fight no longer, and death came. And now the house was empty again, except for the ghost memories of their voices and the ringing of the telephone that was no longer there.

And they were still here, the unmentionable evil of the man and the woman and their mindless disciples. They lived somewhere out there, anywhere; they didn't need a roof over their heads, for they never slept; no food, for they were never hungry. They walked at midnight under the moon, and they were here now—Maskell knew it—outside; waiting in the shadows—he could see them. And escape lay up and above, at the top of a stairway that led upwards into infinity. He had to climb to escape. Climb a stairway that was alive: writhing, twisting, never still; inviting him to climb; withdrawing when he would have set his foot on the first step.

Then somehow he was on it, and climbing, but with something holding him back, his feet trapped as if in a quagmire, his outstretched hands clawing at the empty air. The heart of the house was still pounding, but now no longer outside his head, but inside; inside his skull, forcing it to expand, to swell, to finally split asunder.

And splitting, in a flash of white fire, it sent him falling, arms and legs spread star-fashion, falling into nightmare blackness.

EIGHT

The world beyond the private darkness of his closed lids had been still and quiet for some time now. Sense and reason had slowly returned. The nightmare interlude was over. He had only to open his eyes and he would be ready to take up where he had been forced to leave off when the hallucinations started. Maskell knew who he was and where he was. He was himself again, wholly himself; no distortions, no imaginings. But just for a little while it was good to lie still and let the world outside wash over his privacy of darkness.

He had tried to find some cause for the hallucinations. So vivid, it was difficult to think of them as being nothing but mental images and impressions. And terrifying. His forehead was still damp—he could feel the clammy chill—from that last struggle to climb the staircase, and that nightmare fall into nothingness. Worse than the first time; much worse. And not caused by drugs or some other outside influence, but by something here in the house. Some kind of chiasma. Or perhaps by the very house itself, its very structure. A repository for memories. Every house must be that. But could a place be haunted by memories of a very special kind in such a way that, like a circuit becoming overloaded, from time to time the thing is set in motion, sounds and images being projected into the minds of anyone unfortunate enough to be there at the time?

Now he was thinking gibberish. A short session with Sir John once he was away from this damn place, and between them they'd get at the cause of the trouble. Maskell opened his eyes.

He was lying where he knew he must be lying, at the foot of the stairs. And feeling neither cramped nor uncomfortable for all his head was on the hard wood of the bottom step, and the rest of him sprawled across the hard stone floor of the hall. Daylight still, the hall filled with light; bright, almost dazzling, and that could be accounted for by his eyes having been closed for some time. For how long? He held his arm high above his head. Half past six, by his watch, after some small trouble in focussing.

Sitting up, he straightened out his legs and then pushed himself to his feet, stretching, breathing deeply. He felt better than he had for quite some time. It was as if in some strange way the hallucinations had purged both his mind and his body, leaving both shining and clean. A kind of tapping of hidden reserves under stress; the athletes' second breath.

And like the other time, his mind was functioning smoothly, mechanically. The superefficient, calculating mind to which deciphering a code would be child's play. He reached to his hip. The pocket there was empty. But the sheet of pencilled calculations had been there, and those on which he himself had been working: a wad of paper. They were all gone. While he had been unconscious, for two hours or more by his reckoning, someone had searched him and removed the precious papers. But no cause for worry. On their own, without the bulk coded returns in the briefcase, they would be useless. He felt very confident that the hiding place he had chosen for the case had thwarted any attempts made to find it. All the same, it would be as well to make sure.

It was just as he had left it. Then, standing by the open fuse box, about to push the panel back into place, it occurred to him that the people with whom he was dealing, being the kind of people they were, might at this very moment be spying on him from someplace nearby, having guessed that the first thing he would do on finding the papers gone from his pocket would be to go to check to see if the briefcase had also gone. Which was just what he had done, and so had fallen into their trap and given the place away. Fortunately, he had been astute enough to see through the manoeuvre in time. A new hiding place would have to be found.

Carrying the case back to the house, it struck him that it was a great pity that just at this moment, with his mind, as it had the other time, functioning with the superefficiency of a data-digital-processing machine, he couldn't bring it to bear on the relatively simple problem of breaking down the code. He felt confident that, while it lasted, this new faculty, if presented with the launching-pad information on the sheet of pencilled calculations, along with the contents of the case he was carrying, would produce a positive result in a very short time.

He re-entered the house by way of a french window that he couldn't recall having used before—tall and slender with an elegant gilt-carved frame and an impression of rustling curtain.

No suitable hiding place in the room into which he stepped—oddly, the room with the settee and chairs where he had passed the night. In the hall the case of the grandfather clock was wide enough for his purpose, but seemed too obvious a place. The kitchen with its bulky impedimenta of range and cupboards and recesses seemed much more hopeful. But none of the cupboards was wide enough, none of the recesses concealing enough. And so, frustration rising, it would have to be upstairs. Maskell went back into the hall. How he could have missed it before he didn't know, but there it was, lying on the floor at the foot of the stairs where it must have fallen out of his pocket when unconscious—a wad of folded papers. And now here he had everything needed to break the code.

This time he chose the kitchen, the warmest room in the house and, although one wouldn't have thought so, by far the largest. And here too was a substitute for his office desk—the kitchen table, space in which to spread himself. Drawing up a chair he sat down.

The documents from the briefcase here, on his right, piled high, higher—there seemed no end to them; each folder he brought out to add to the pile must be the last, but always there was one more left in the case. But at long last they were all out and ready, and here at his left hand was the providential sheet of pencilled calculations; and in the middle, set out with military precision, working paper and pens and pencils. Everything was ready. He knew, *knew*, exactly how to set about breaking the code. But his mind had become a blank.

He stared down at a column of figures and was unable to read meaning of any kind in them. He concentrated until the figures blurred and went out of focus. He pressed the heel of his palm against his forehead and willed the figures to make sense. He concentrated until sweat broke out beneath his palm and the figures became a column of ants that went marching off the paper and across the table to the distant sound of drums. The drumbeat echoed inside his head, grew, became words, became words in shining letters on a tape that glided between the front of his mind and the backs of his eyes like a news sign atop a New York skyscraper. One million, it read, the figures of disaster—two million, three million, more—

While he was sitting here, helpless, back there in the other world, the real world, that was the city, Agnew, with a dozen pairs of arms, and hands on each, and still not enough fingers for all the pies from which the plums must be taken, was slowly but surely lining his own pockets at the expense of Saturn.

One million, two million, three million, more—Saturn smashed to smithereens, and Earlam brought toppling to the dust.

More than that . . . enough to undermine financial dealings on the 'Change and start a landslide that would dwarf the Wall Street disaster. Enough to shatter the very country itself, for a country is only a matter of finance, and bring ruin to millions of people.

One million, two million, three million, more— A rhythm set up in his brain, click-jogging like the wheels of a train; a crescendo of bursting, silent sound—unbearable. And then, quite suddenly, peace. And from out of the blessed relief of that peace, a woman's soft throaty voice saying: "Boyd. Boyd Maskell."

She must be standing in the darkness by the door. That was where the voice came from, so, for all there was nothing to see at first, that was where she must be. As he strained with narrowed eyes, so part of the shadows became darker than the rest, took outline, took shape, hardened . . . the legs first—long and incredibly slender and shining black nylon. And then, his gaze rising, the sudden pure shining whiteness of arms and shoulders and breasts. And then the face, but for some reason, the features indistinct, barely defined, visible only as a pale oval, with dark melting shadow above for the hair, and smoky slanting pools that were eyes, and the dark curved richness that was her mouth. A small face under a fringe of hair—that was as much as he was able to establish with any certainty. He willed her to come closer, move out of the shadow and out into the light so that he could see her clearly.

He leaned forward in his chair, hearing himself ask in a voice that belonged to someone else: "Who are you?"

Her husky voice was temptation itself. "You know who I am, Boyd." And she mimicked: "And who are you?"

Teasing him. There was no evil in her, as he had once pictured—but that had been in a dream—now he was awake. No evil, only goodness, all goodness.

"You seem to know who I am without my having to tell you," he said, and leaned forward still more, demanding: "Come nearer so I can see you."

The tantalising laugh again. "But I like it here, Boyd. I like the night and the darkness. You know that. It was dark the first time you saw me, remember? Out there in the night and the darkness and the moonlight. And then again, the next time we met . . . Do you remember that as well, Boyd? Or have you forgotten?"

No, he hadn't forgotten; he would never forget. He wanted to tell her so, but for some reason the words refused to come.

Instead: "Who are you?" he asked again, and put his hands on the arms of the chair, trying to push himself up. But he must have become stiff from having sat there so long, working, for there wasn't enough strength in his arms to take his weight and he had to give up the attempt, sinking back into the clammy leather.

The girl—he could tell she was only a girl by the bell tone of her voice and her figure—laughed again, mocking, amused by his efforts. "Poor Boyd. I thought you wanted to take a closer look at me."

"If you won't tell me who you are, tell me your name," he begged desperately.

"Why do you want to know?"

"Because—" For the life of him he couldn't think of a good

enough reason to offer. "I want to have something to think of you by," he said lamely. And then that suddenly became important: that he should have a name for her for the afterwards when she would be gone.

"They call me—" she started, and then a breeze found its way in from outside, and found a chink in the lamp, causing the flame to splutter, sending shadows and shapes in alternate patterns dancing madly, redly round the walls. And just for a moment, so it seemed to him, the girl became part of the dance, that was off whirling with the rest. Then the flame settled again and the shadows became still and she was standing unmoving by the door, smiling—he could sense rather than see her teasing smile. And this time when he attempted to push himself up out of the chair he succeeded, and was wonderfully on his feet and moving towards her, eyes straining to catch that first clear glimpse of her face, which would be the one he would fold away in the private place of his memory for all time. But as he advanced, so she, seeming to float rather than walk, moved backwards before him, laughing all the time, backwards through the door and into the denser shadows of the hall, in danger of becoming one of them.

He snatched up a lamp. Her teasing laughter mocked his efforts as he turned, holding in front of him, high, a holy symbol that would drive away the evil darkness. As it drove away the shadows of the hall, leaving nothing behind but emptiness. She had vanished with them, the girl of black nylon and scarlet satin and shining white flesh.

"Where are you?" he called up the stairs from the foot of the stairs, and his voice went winging away into some place of vast emptiness and there gathered to itself an echo, and that echo came rumbling back, beating like the wheels of a train—one million, two million, three million, four . . . the litany of disaster. Five million, six million, seven million, more. The rhythm of ruin. Ten million, more . . .

Inside his head, that pounding beat. Imagination making use of his own pulse beat, magnifying it, playing tricks with it. As the lamp was again playing tricks with the shadows, flaring redly for no reason at all, dark shapes careering wildly round the walls;

walls that seemed to be closing in on him from all sides. And from a long way away, a small, lost, distant voice calling: "Where are you, Boyd? Boyd?" Her voice calling: "Boyd, where are you?"

Surely not his hand, not these his thin white fingers clamped about the brass base of the lamp—skeletal, white-knuckled, articulated like the legs of a shrunken white spider. And not his face, by its feel, by the feel of parchment flesh drawn tightly into a grimace of death over sunken cheeks and projecting bone. He could only sense the new contours, not see them. Nor, oddly, feel them, because both his hands were full—the lamp in one, and in the other—he couldn't remember how it had come to be there—a telephone, shining black, an old-fashioned telephone with tulip mouthpiece and cradled receiver, and its cord trailing back into the darkness like an umbilical cord. He let the telephone fall to the floor. Now he had a hand with which to feel the new contours of his face, but he could still not see them for there was no mirror. No mirror anywhere in this cursed house. A house without a mirror . . .

There was a mirror, he remembered, on the wall at the top of the staircase. And having climbed to it, marvelled at such elegance in such surroundings. Oval glass; ornate Florentine gilt; baroque; silks and satins and powdered wigs and blue brocade and tinkling spinets . . . Mirror, mirror, on the wall—

Lighted, someway, from above, and so just for a moment a little strange, but still his face, that face in the oval glass. Not shrunken, distorted, as he had feared by its feel, but as it had always been—narrow features; soft, almost feminine lines—a visionary's face, not that of a hard, knife-edge, on-the-ball executive. There had been times when that deceptive appearance had served him in good stead. Soft wing of dark-bronze hair silky on poet's white brow. And here he was wasting time gazing Narcissus-like at his own face when he should be searching the house for the girl.

He held the lamp aloft. On either side, the passages were empty. "Where are you?" he called despairingly.

The light was failing, the flame in the lamp shrinking down.

There was plenty of oil—he shook it, hearing the splish-splash in the reservoir. He turned the flame up. Darkness came dropping.

He was lying on his back on something cold and hard, opening his eyes, where they had already been open, to look up to where an oval of whiteness floated in a pool of grey mist. The mist thinned. The oval became a face. A face he recognised. Fairfield's anxious face, and Fairfield's troubled voice saying: "This is getting to be too much of a good thing, finding you flaked out like this every time I turn my back. And what the hell have you been up to this time?"

NINE

It was daylight, bright daylight, and that was something Maskell found confusing; trying to work out in his mind which day this light belonged to—if indeed a night had gone by and this was the new day, or if he had only dreamed that the night had passed, making this now still the old day.

Propped on one elbow, he asked of Fairfield's inverted face: "What day is it?"

"You are in a bad way. Tuesday it is, old sport; still Tuesday."

It had been a dream. Sadly, not real. He had wanted so much for the girl to have been real.

"And what do you think you are doing down there?" Fairfield asked.

"Down there" being the stone flags at the foot of the stairs, the exact spot on which he had woken once before. No, Maskell corrected himself, only dreamed he had woken. None of it had been real. And yet it had seemed so at the time. Real, and sensible. But already reason and reality were peeling away like the skins off an onion. Unnatural, childish, his conversation with the girl. The girl. . . . She had stood—there—in the shadows of the doorway. He had dropped the telephone—and how could he have thought its sudden appearance sane and sensible?—there. The mirror had been on the wall—he turned to look up the stairs at the blank wall at the top—up there. And there was no need to go into the kitchen to know there would be no papers littering the table. That part of the dream had been the most real. And still was now, even though he was awake again. Looking back on it was just like looking back on an episode that had actually happened. So real, in fact, that Maskell pushed himself to his feet and went into the kitchen to make sure.

Fairfield joined him, as he brooded over the empty table—empty, that is, apart from the used beer cans—silently going about the business of stirring the fire to life, filling the kettle, reaching down two clean cups. "A cup of tea'll do us both good." And, certainly very genuinely concerned: "Like the other time, was it? You know—like the other time?"

Maskell knew what he meant. "Worse than the other time." It helped, he found, to talk about it, describe what had happened. It helped nail down the dream for what it was, part of the hallucination.

"How the bloody hell did they manage it?" Fairfield wanted to know. "Get the dope to you—you know? It's got to be that. Got to be. There's just no other answer."

"I don't think I can take much more of it," Maskell said simply. "I'm afraid of reaching the stage where I won't be able to distinguish between reality and hallucination."

"It'll never come to that." Fairfield poured tea. "Here, get this down you. Think back. Try to think back. Before it started, you know—what was the last thing you had to eat or drink?"

"Brian was here. I asked him about that. I thought at first that what he was trying to say was that he'd somehow managed to give me some sort of drug. But he said he hadn't, and I could tell from his face he was telling the truth. He's a gentle person, I'm sure of that. I don't believe he'd harm anyone. And I don't think he has enough intelligence to be able to lie without giving himself away."

"If he didn't fix you, then someone else did." Fairfield was very sure of that. "How's it going now?"

It was going reasonably well. Maskell, finding comfort in the tea he was drinking, essayed a small flash of humour. "I'll live." A thought occurred to him and he reached behind to pat his hip pocket. The papers were still there.

Fairfield, spotting the movement, guessed at its significance. "You still reckon it's all part of a scheme to get at your private papers?"

"I'm not so sure now." Maskell put his cup down. "It could equally well be somebody's scheme to make me seem unfitted to remain in my job so that someone else can step into my shoes."

"You mean, all this for the sake of a bloody job?" The other was frankly disbelieving. "Come off it, son. No job's that important in my book."

"It's not so much the job itself—although there's a lot of people would give a great deal for the pay and position—but what the job could mean. It's pretty well unique. Whoever occupies the post is in the position of knowing very many stock market fluctuations in advance. If I had a mind to it, I could make myself a great deal of money. I don't, because I'm trusted not to, and because any profit I made would be at the expense of my employers."

"But somebody else might not have your scruples," Fairfield mused. "I'm beginning to get the picture. And you really think that's what it's all about?" By his expression he was genuinely anxious to hear Maskell's opinion.

"I do, and I can have a stab at guessing who's behind it. I mean the big wheel himself, the man behind the scenes, not the underling who would step into my shoes. He'll just be a puppet. Pearson Agnew. I may have mentioned him before."

"Ay." Fairfield rubbed the side of his long white nose. His gypsy-black hair, more matted now than merely uncombed, flopped untidily over his forehead when he nodded. "Something high up in your mob. Look, I don't know much about this finance lark, but if you're right, and he does get away with it, won't your bosses know what he's up to the minute he starts the profit-making?"

"He won't do anything himself," Maskell explained. "He'll use another puppet, probably several of them. He runs his own company. Biddulph Electronics." And at the other's involuntary catching of the breath: "You know them?"

"I've heard of them. I don't know them."

But to Maskell it was transparently obvious that the name had meant something more to Fairfield than that. The first false note struck since his arrival back from—

Maskell asked: "Where did you vanish to over in the village?"

"Yes." The other rubbed the side of his nose again, a habit that could denote uncertainty. "I was wondering when you'd get round to that. Well, we were up the church tower, you know? And you said you saw something or somebody—"

"Go on," Maskell said when Fairfield paused.

"Well, I could see nothing, but you obviously could, so I went for a closer look, didn't I? Thought it best to slip away on my tod without saying anything. You'd been looking at one of the cottages that stood on its own. That's where I went." Fairfield made a face. "Nothing there. The place was worse than just empty, it wasn't far off being a ruin. Anyway, I went round the back, just to be sure. Thought I was on to something at first. A path. Only it didn't go anywhere. I followed it a piece, leading right out into the middle of nowhere. Then it began to get a bit dicey. Even with my trusty staff I don't trust the muck out there. Swallow you up as soon as look. So I turned back.

"And I wasn't going to mention this, but I will. On the way back I had myself a narrowish shave. As I was passing the cottage I thought I saw something move behind one of the windows—well, where the windows used to be. Like someone moving. So I went to have a look. Not a sausage. Then I heard footsteps out at the back. Or fancied I did. Maybe this bloody place is getting on my nerves too. Anyway, I went to have a look. And just as I stepped out of the back door—"

He tugged at the roll neck of his thick grey sweater. When it wouldn't come down far enough for his purpose he pulled it up over his head to expose a chest mat of black hair made all the more obvious by contrast with the white of his arms and shoulders. But not unblemished white, one shoulder at least. The large purple bruise on the left one was what he had wanted Maskell to see. "If I hadn't heard it giving a grating sound and moved a bit sharpish, it would have copped me smack across the back of the head, which, let me tell you, could have been very nasty indeed. Chunk of window framework, it was. Must have gradually weathered loose until me opening the back door was enough to bring it down."

"You're sure it was only an accident?"

By Fairfield's reception of the question he had already considered and disposed of the alternative.

"Who would want to do *me* any harm?" he asked simply, and reached for the teapot. Something rattled in his trouser pocket. "What the devil—? Oh, I'd forgotten about these. Interesting, the things one comes across." He tipped them on the table. "Found them by that path I was telling you about. I know Scotland is the land of grouse and pheasant and deer, and the place is likely to be knee-deep in empty cartridge cases, but I know what sort of cartridges they use in shotguns, and they're not like these. I'd say these have come out of a pretty hefty rifle. Although I'm not all that well up in this sort of thing."

Neither was Maskell. He stirred the half-dozen brass cylinders with a disinterested finger. "Perhaps they use rifles as well as shotguns on the moors."

"I doubt it." Fairfield swept them back into his pocket and then upended the teapot over his empty cup. "Muck," he observed dispassionately of the brown trickle. "What wouldn't I give for a bottle of what this bloody country's supposed to be famous for." His wandering gaze found the empty cans, lingered on their labels. "You might have told me you'd found some beer on your travels."

"I've had rather more important things on my mind."

"Ay, I reckon you have at that. Like getting away from here. If you've had any ideas on the subject, I'll go along with them."

Maskell looked at his watch. After all the things that had happened, it was still not yet half past five. It felt like he had spent a lifetime in the house. "You said earlier that you had a map and then burned it," he said. "Can you remember which is the nearest place of any size to where we are? Or any place at all?"

The other made a face. "To be honest, I'm not all that hot on maps, even when I've got one in front of me. The one I had, I didn't study it all that much. About all I can remember of it now was this bloody big empty space called Rannoch Moor covered with lots of little green lines with tufts growing out of them, which is probably the way they mark bogs and that sort of thing. There was a town called Oban. Which way are we facing now?" He rubbed the bridge of his nose. "To the south." He pointed back over his shoulder. "Thataway. About thirty miles. And if you're thinking of hitting the road right now, well, there's about three hours of daylight left, and to go walking out there without any roads or paths, you take my word, you need broad daylight."

Which, Maskell felt, was true enough. All the same—"I'm not all that keen on spending another night here."

"No." Fairfield massaged his injured shoulder. "Just between you and me, I'm not too enamoured of the prospect myself. But what have you? If you've an alternative, I'm your man."

But it was obvious there was no alternative. Maskell still clutched for straws. "And Oban is the nearest place? You're sure of that? There's not even a hamlet we could make for, no matter what size?"

"I've thought about it, don't you worry. No, there's this empty space"—Fairfield drew it in the air with his finger—"with Oban down here and Kirkmalcolm in the middle and Balla-whatsits-name up here. Oban's the nearest to us."

Maskell went to stand by the window. Flat and spreading as the moorland was out there, it was hard to imagine the nearest place as being thirty miles away.

"We could take it in turns," Fairfield suggested from behind. "Dossing down. I watch while you sleep, then you for me. And we'll have to be a bit canny, as the locals say, about what we eat and drink. Just in case they have any more ideas about trips—maybe sending both of us off on them next time." And when Maskell turned to look at him: "At the risk of sounding monotonous, hallucinations just don't happen on their own, you know. Not unless you're already halfway—" He broke off, embarrassed. "This bloody place is enough to get on anyone's wick." He changed the subject quickly. "Have you finished the work you're supposed to be doing, or is there still some left?"

Maskell stared at him. "What work do you mean?" he asked suspiciously.

"How the hell do I know? Whatever it was you were doing when I first showed up here. You told me you were working, remember?"

Maskell did remember, and regretted his display of suspicion. He had been working, trying to break the code. He stared down at the table. In the dream, breaking it had been the easiest thing under the sun. And the method he had used—it was still there, at the back of his mind, just out of reach, so sensible a system that it was hard to realise it had been only a dream. But that was all it had been, and awake, there was no special system, no short-cut. And it would be just waste of time now to carry on with his old hit-and-miss method.

"I've finished what I was doing," he said.

Oddly, Fairfield seemed concerned about that, as if he had a personal stake in the thing. "You're sure about that?" And, hastily: "I'm not trying to butt in or anything—don't get me wrong. Only the impression I got from what you told me was that the work you'd brought with you was very important. I mean, I wouldn't like to think that what's been happening here has stopped you doing something important." He floundered. "You know what I mean."

"I'm not sure I do." Maskell regarded him steadily. "Why should you be concerned about my work?"

"I'm not. Oh, for God's sake, forget it." Fairfield came to his feet. "We'll spend a cosy evening together and then go to bed in shifts." He grinned briefly. "I didn't intend that to be funny. Me, I've been sleeping in what I stand up in. Crude, but saves on the baggage. I'll make up a fire in the room where the settee and chairs are."

In the dream, Maskell recalled, the briefcase had still been safe in its hiding place. He wondered if it was still there now. Its contents may have lost their usefulness so far as he was concerned, but their safety was still very much his responsibility.

"I'll take a look round outside," he said.

Fairfield, collecting sticks in one hand and coal scuttle in the other, raised his eyebrows slightly. "Fair enough. And I'll see about a fire. Feels like it might get coolish when the Scottish sun goes down."

About to open the front door, Maskell heard the other's exclamation and turned to find the cause. Fairfield had stopped in the kitchen doorway. He shrugged a little sheepishly at Maskell's look of enquiry. "Thought I saw something in the window.

Could have been a face." Putting down his load, he went back into the kitchen. Maskell waited until he returned, shaking his head. "Nothing. Like I said, this bloody place is getting on my nerves too."

Maskell walked quickly to the larger of the two outhouses. The briefcase was still there, seemingly untouched. About to replace the panel, he changed his mind, tucking the briefcase under his arm to carry it back to the house and there spread its contents across the coffee table in the lounge. Carrying on with their original routine appraisal would at least be something to do to help the time pass.

Fairfield grunted himself upright from putting a match to the fire. He nodded in the direction of the papers. "They have a familiar look to them. Spend most of my working life sitting at a desk covered with stuff like that." He stirred the growing fire with his foot. "Feel like eating now or later?"

Later, Maskell told him after consideration, and the other nodded agreeably and, having been reminded, went off to fill and clean the oil lamps. "Talk about the bleeding Middle Ages."

Silver twilight settled into purple dusk, and after a while the moon rose, flooding the world with clear cold light. A half moon, Maskell saw when he turned to look through the window, sailing across a sky from which most of the clouds had disappeared.

Working, the time passed quickly enough. He was surprised when Fairfield, who had been dozing in an armchair, pulled close to the fire, stretched himself awake to announce that it was ten past nine and how about giving him a hand to open a can of beans or two. Maskell asked for five minutes to finish the report he was working on. It occurred to him, when Fairfield, carrying one of the lamps, had gone to the kitchen, that it was quite some time since he had heard either the telephone ringing or the voices. Not, in fact, since the second hallucination.

In the kitchen, Fairfield set his lamp on the table, adjusted the wick to give a better light and then turned, hands on hips, to consider preparations for a meal. The back door, he then noticed, was wide open. And he was as sure as could be that earlier, when he had stepped outside to see if anyone had been looking in at the window, he had closed it behind him on his return. Blown open by the wind? But there wasn't even a breeze. So somebody had come along and opened it. He rubbed the side of his nose thoughtfully. One of two people, was his guess. The loony type or—

From outside a man's voice called softly but clearly: "You, there—"

Startlement made Fairfield jump, made his voice loud. "Who the hell's that?"

"Quietly," the voice said with some urgency. "Come out here; I want to talk to you."

Come into my parlour . . . But Fairfield, for all he had only a very vague idea as to the ownership of the voice, still felt fairly certain he knew what it wanted to talk about and why it preferred to talk outside. And so, after only a moment's hesitation, he accepted the invitation.

Moments later, Maskell, closing the folder on which he had been working, was brought to his feet by the loud and anguished cry. A shout for help, no doubt about that; Fairfield's voice, and it had come from the direction of the kitchen.

Fairfield was still on his feet when Maskell burst into the room, but swaying, eyes closed, one hand supporting himself against the table, the other pressed to the side of his forehead, blood trickling between his fingers.

As Maskell ran to help him, so he leaned slowly forward, his hand sliding off the edge of the table, his knees buckling, to collapse, unconscious on the floor.

TEN

There was no one in sight outside, the world bright with moon-light. Maskell closed the back door, returned to the grate the poker he had hurriedly snatched up to serve as a weapon, then knelt at Fairfield's side.

The blood had come from a ragged gash where the skin had been broken at the centre of a patch of already darkening bruise. Not a deep gash, he was relieved to see; it had already stopped bleeding. He used a strip of linen ripped from one of the tea towels and soaked in cold water to wash the blood away. Fairfield stirred back into consciousness as he was patting dry with the rest of the towel. With Maskell's help—"Take it easy"—he managed to push himself up into a sitting position with his back against one of the table legs. But that seemed as far as he could get. His face was ashen, and when he put up his hand to explore the bruise, his fingers were shaking. It cost him an obvious effort to twist round to peer in the direction of the back door. "I don't suppose you saw—"

"No." Maskell, still crouching, shook his head. "I had a look outside. No sign."

"Bastard," Fairfield said softly, closed his eyes and went limp. Maskell was just in time to catch his head and lower it to the floor. With vague memories of camping first aid he soaked his piece of towel in cold water again, and this time used it on the unconscious man's forehead. When there was no reaction, he came upright again, completely at a loss.

It didn't seem right, couldn't be doing him any good, to leave him sprawled like that on the bare floor. He would be better in bed but, tallish and well-built, too heavy to carry, getting him up the stairs was out of the question. It would have to be the settee in the other room.

Maskell hooked his hands under the unconscious man's armpits and dragged him, a dead weight, even heavier than he had thought, across the hall, his heels scraping along the floor and bumping over the cracks between the stone flags, into the lounge. First his lolling head and shoulders onto the settee, then, with a straining effort, the rest of him, and Maskell straightened, breathing heavily, sweat shining on his narrow forehead.

It seemed surprising to him that Fairfield had remained unconscious through all that bouncing and jerking. Suspicious, he used his thumbs to carefully peel back the closed lids, something he had never tried doing before, but had seen done on television. It seemed sensible to assume that if only the whites of the eyes showed, no pupil, and there was no fluttering of the lids, then the patient wasn't faking but was well and truly out.

As Fairfield most certainly was now—still marble-faced, and breathing deeply and noisily—what was the word?—stertorously. Again, with long-ago memories of always keeping the patient warm, not that it was all that cold in the room, the fire not quite dead, he went upstairs, lamp held high, to collect a blanket and, as an afterthought, a pillow. To complete the thing he brought the tea-towel cold compress from the kitchen to lay it, neatly folded, across the pallid forehead, having to push the mass of heavy black hair aside.

And that was about all he could do. He didn't think Fairfield could be badly hurt, otherwise he wouldn't have come round for those few minutes. And for all the throaty breathing, he didn't think there was likely to be any chance of concussion from a blow to the side of the forehead.

The lamp flickered and dimmed a little. Maskell hurried to turn up the wick and bring it bright again. Plenty of oil: it had not long since been filled. At least he was sure of light of a kind. Stirring up the fire and adding coal to the red embers, he wondered if he ought to make something to drink to have ready when Fairfield came round. But there was no way of telling how long that might be. And in any event, it didn't seem right to leave him here alone, even just to go to the kitchen.

The only sound in the world was Fairfield's laboured breathing. The house seemed all the more silent and still by contrast.

Bright moonlight outside still—Maskell stood by the window, each small pane of glass aglow—the sky still clear, the silvered world empty, no weird figures standing by the copse of flattened, cutout trees. Bright enough the sailing half moon for him to read his watch by its light. Twenty past nine. Long past his usual dinnertime. An eternity, it seemed, since he had last eaten, but he was conscious of no great desire for food, particularly the kind at his disposal here.

And then a certain numbness seemed to lift from his mind so that for the first time since Fairfield had been attacked he found himself wondering who had stuck the blow and why. A mistake, he thought at first; the attacker had mistaken his victim, had really intended it to be the same person who had been on the receiving end of all the other attacks that had been made; those all psychological, this the first physical one.

But then, upon reflection—his mind functioning normally again, capable of reasoning—he saw how it couldn't have been a mistake after all, that the attack must have been intended for Fairfield. For there had been plenty of light on the scene—lamplight in the kitchen, bright moonlight outside. The intruder could have had no difficulty at all in identifying his victim.

But why Fairfield, he puzzled, who himself was part of the conspiracy? When thieves fall out—something like that? He didn't think it likely. And why was he so sure that the unconscious man was part of the conspiracy? Because of the voices and the telephone that he had pretended not to hear. Maskell refused to even consider the possibility that Fairfield might not have been acting after all, and might really be what he had made himself out to be, an innocent bystander. A very disturbing train of thought, one best abandoned in favour of something more sensible. Like, Who had the assailant been?

He didn't think it was Brian. From what little he had had to do with him—and he was somewhat surprised now to find he had developed quite a soft spot for the feeble-minded youth—he couldn't imagine him doing such a thing. A snap judgement based on Brian's gentle appearance and way of speaking. But he had heard it said that mild-tempered, mentally deficient people were very often unpredictably violent. All the same, a much more likely candidate was the man in the black cloak. Maskell smiled to himself at his mental use of the barnstorming title. It was no use trying to guess what had motivated the attack.

Fairfield hadn't stirred. But his breathing seemed less laboured, more natural. Another good sign was that most of the colour had returned to his face. Not an overintelligent face. Hands on the cold leather back of the settee, Maskell gazed down dispassionately at the motionless figure. Another snap judgement—he pulled a small face—and like the first, quite capable of being completely wrong. As he had thought on first seeing Fairfield—a lifetime ago—it was quite possible he was underestimating what lay behind that long, loose-mouthed, thick-lipped face. One thing was for certain, he assured himself: whatever was going on here, Fairfield was in it up to his neck—*had* to be—please God let him be . . . The alternative was too terrifying to consider.

Somewhere in the house, someone closed a door. Maskell distinctly heard the unmistakable and quite loud sound. Not from upstairs, the source of the other sounds, but from the direction of the kitchen. The dividing door between hall and kitchen, he guessed, and, another poker in hand—this little more than an ornament, much smaller and lighter than that from the kitchen range—he went quickly into the hall, dark apart from the rectangle of spilled light from his room, his own shadow, weapon in hand, splashed threatening and grotesque across the reddish rectangle.

He couldn't remember closing the kitchen door behind him when dragging Fairfield out—he couldn't have done it, unless he had reached back with a hooked foot—but it was closed now, a thin ribbon of light showing beneath. He listened at its panels, ineffectual weapon held ready, hearing nothing but the faster-than-usual thudding of his own heart. Turning the knob he crashed the door open.

The room was empty, the light coming from the lamp on the table where he had left it, but the back door stood open, and that he did distinctly remember closing before attending to Fairfield.

He looked outside, not stepping beyond the threshold. The moon still sailed high and clear, but clouds had gathered along the horizon and were coiling darkly upwards, fanciful, slow-moving monsters with silvered veins. But on the ground, with no breeze to stir the leaves, nothing moved. Whatever had caused the sound he had heard had gone again. The assailant returned to look for his victim's body? Hardly likely after such a longish interval, Maskell felt, and stepped back into the kitchen away from the menace of the night, closing the door behind him and collecting the lamp on his way back to the lounge.

To the empty lounge, the settee bare, Fairfield gone. The blanket lay some distance away, as if impatiently tossed aside; the pillow was on the floor alongside the settee, clearly dragged there by Fairfield's head; the strip of cloth was over by the other door, the start of a paper chase indicating which way Fairfield had been taken—taken, because it seemed impossible he should have recovered enough to be able to move on his own accord in such a short space of time.

Through the door, lamp held high, and into the next room, and there the next clue: one of the french windows stood open. But outside, the same story as before, with no sign of anything or anyone. A dozen ways the trail might lead from here. And pointless now, with clouds ready to sweep the moonlight aside, to try to find and follow any signs that might indicate which direction to take. It seemed obvious to Maskell now that the sound of the door closing had been a deliberate sound, a ruse to draw him away, leaving Fairfield alone long enough for him to be abducted. He closed the french window—a gesture only, with no means of securing it—and with the lamp to show him the way, returned to the lounge to quite calmly gather up cloth, blanket and pillow and pile them at one end of the settee.

He was surprised at himself for the placid way in which he had taken, was taking, Fairfield's being attacked and then his disappearance. An unnatural attitude, he supposed. Fatalistic—was that the word? Take things as they come and remain detached from the world around. A not unpleasant frame of mind, he discovered upon reflection; and with it, a sense almost of power. I am above all these petty events . . . a reaction of sorts. Or perhaps a kind of aftermath of the hallucinations. Whatever the cause, it was a sensible way to be. Flying off into hysterics wouldn't help. Take things steady. Sooner or later, whoever was behind this campaign of incomprehensibles would make a slip and give himself away. Every campaign had its weak point. Lesson Three of High Finance. Lesson One was trust no man, not even your own father.

Maskell stirred the fire with the toy poker, arranged the two lamps to give maximum illumination, and then set about collecting the papers he had earlier been working on to help while away the time.

Not all that far away, Fairfield opened his eyes. He had been verging on full consciousness for some time, vaguely aware of possessing different and varied sources of pain and discomfort: a tightness under his armpits; a constriction in his chest; and, worst of all, a kind of continual jerking of his whole body that had caused his head to pound painfully and violently.

But now all that had ceased, and so had a sensation of movement that had been associated with a banging against the backs of his legs and thighs. He was still now; the world was still and dark, and he was lying on his back on something that seemed neither fluid nor solid, but something of each. Not uncomfortable, and so he was content to lie there and slowly recover and savour the stillness—until the light came, seeping through a thinning of the clouds, filtered moonlight that showed him that what he had taken to be two trees, one growing on each side of him, were not trees at all, but—

The man—if it was a man—he had seen before, but only from a distance, recognising him then by his strange clothes, his flowing, voluminous black cloak. Now he towered into the night sky, silhouetted against the coiling clouds, looking down from his pillared black height with eyes that were empty black pools in a white face with painted-on hair.

And on Fairfield's other side, the tree there had become a woman he had never seen before, but was able to recognise even in that light from Maskell's description of sequinned scarlet bodice, long black-nyloned legs and alabaster arms and shoulders. Ageless, her face shadowed and featureless, she bent slowly over him, arms reaching down with hands spread in a strange gesture of benediction.

And it was then he became aware that the ground on which he lay was alive, moving slowly beneath him, reaching out, sending clinging tentacles creeping over arms and legs, dragging him gently but remorsely down . . .

Lamp in hand, Maskell went to the kitchen. From somewhere he had found an appetite. But he was not too hungry to spare time to light the fire yet again to heat up the contents of some of the stacks of cans instead of eating them cold and greasy. And it was something to do. Not yet ten, and a long sleepless night ahead. Sleepless, because it wouldn't be a very clever thing to do to close his eyes for any length of time. It was only assumption on his part that Fairfield had indeed been the intended victim. It could have been a mistake after all, and his attackers—for some reason he now found himself thinking in terms of more than one—having disposed of his unconscious body, might return for the real victim.

For all the fire was burning up, it had become rather cold in the kitchen. He carried a plate and some pieces of cutlery through to the now empty coffee table in the warmer lounge. Another journey back across the twilight zone of the shadowy, echoing hall, and during the few minutes he had been gone, someone had come into the kitchen. His back was towards the doorway, but there was no need to see his face. The white shirt and faded blue jeans were enough. Brian stood by the sink, rolling up his sleeves and not waiting until he had finished that job before reaching to turn on the tap.

Maskell pulled himself up in time, stopping dead on the threshold, afraid of venturing further in case of frightening his visitor away before they had even had chance to exchange words, knowing from the past how timid he was, how afraid of being near to anyone.

But it seemed that with the attraction of the sink full of accumulated dirty dishes, there was no need for caution. Brian, who must surely have heard the sound of footsteps crossing the stone-flagged hall, didn't even turn round, so engrossed was he in the business of dealing with the dishes. The water steamed, still hot from earlier fires. From somewhere he had found washing-up liquid, from somewhere else a dishcloth. Fascinated by the slow, deliberate movements, Maskell watched a cup being held up, turned, foam-dripping—a television commercial—to make sure every last speck of dried coffee had been removed, set carefully down on the draining board. Then up with a plate . . .

It would be so easy to startle him, to scare him away.

"Thank you for helping me, Brian," Maskell said quietly, conversationally. "Do you like washing up?"

Just for a moment the thin shoulders tensed. Then they relaxed again. Their owner didn't bother to turn round.

"Not very much," Brian replied, putting the plate to drain and picking up another cup. "I used to wash up lots. Lots of them, all of them. That was what I used to do. All of them. Oh—ever such a lot." The cup was set to drain. Now came a tumbler. "I don't wash up now, though. Not so much. Selena does it most times. I don't mind."

Selena . . . Maskell exhaled sharply. Selena . . . It had to be her. It was her kind of name. Standing in the shadows, smiling at him, teasing, provocative. Selena. And this halfwitted youth with his arms up to the elbows in dishwater knew all about her, who she was, where she came from, where she was living.

"Does Selena like washing dishes?" Maskell asked.

Brian, inspecting a knife, considered the question with gravity. "Not much," he finally decided.

"Perhaps she doesn't like getting her clothes wet. She wears very nice clothes, doesn't she, Brian? Very special clothes?"

A spoon was added to the pile on the draining board. The sink was getting empty. When it was empty, would the dishwasher just up and go? Maskell thought that very likely, and fought an agony of impatience, asking again: "Selena wears very special clothes, doesn't she, Brian?"

"S'lena bought me this shirt," Brian said with pride, letting the water out of the sink. "And my trousers. Oh, an' everything." He reached for a towel.

Maskell tried again. "Is Selena your sister?"

"Sister . . ." Brian thought about that. It seemed that when his hands were occupied his mind wasn't nearly so likely to butterfly off at a tangent as when they were still. "Like in a hospital." Now he had remembered. "I've been in a hospital. Oh—ever such a long time ago . . ."

"Not in a hospital," Maskell said with a patience he was far from feeling. "Like brother and sister, you know? That kind of sister. Is Selena your sister like that?"

It didn't work. Brian, drying now, and carrying the dried pieces item by careful item to the shelves, there reassembling them in their former incomprehensible maniac pattern, considered the question and was nonplussed.

Maskell tried another approach. "Is she here with you now, Brian?"

The other nodded vigorously, still not turning round. "She's always with me, Selena is." He balanced a large dinner plate on an inverted egg cup. "With me and Sevin."

Sevin? *Sevin?* What sort of name was that?

"Who is Sevin?" Maskell asked.

"Sevin's—oh—very clever." A cup was set on top of the plate to complete that segment of the pattern. Brian's voice sank, took on an air of awe. "Sevin can do things other people can't."

A moment of puzzlement, a groping for something familiar, then understanding came. It had to be . . . The name and the costume were both just right. A conjurer, a stage magician. Fluttering dove from silk scarf; bouquet of paper flowers from the folds of the black cloak; white poodle from the empty basket held by the lady assistant. Magician and his assistant. Sevin and Selena. That would explain the costumes. But not why they had seen fit to wander about the moors in the middle of the night wearing those same stage costumes.

Unless—and another inspiration—they had been hired to do precisely that, to create a situation for which any watcher would be unable to find sensible explanations. But that didn't explain Brian's presence. Mentally deficient, yes, but nothing more. Disturbing, perhaps, but certainly not in any way frightening or confusing.

But perhaps they had had no choice but to bring him with them. Sevin, his father, and Selena, his sister. It could be that way. He wished to God he could ask simple questions and get simple, intelligent replies.

But Brian had now almost finished; the shelves were almost full again. And Maskell, apart from having discovered her name, was no nearer finding out who and what the girl was than he had been at the start. And why, for God's sake, he wondered, with all the other things going on all round, did it seem so important to learn all he could about her? It seemed impossible that the fascination she held for him should have stemmed from that one brief moonlight glimpse when not even her face had been visible. Or maybe the dream had been the start. The chicken and the egg . . . Was he intrigued by her because of the dream, or had he dreamed about her because of some subconscious attraction she had come to hold for him?

Selena . . . Selena what? Or perhaps that was only a stage name. Of course it was only a stage name—it had that sort of ring. Then why the devil doesn't Brian call her by her proper name?

Brian said in the tones of a mischievous child conveying a secret: "I'm not supposed to be out at all tonight. He said I wasn't to go out. But I did. I crept out when S'lena wasn't looking." He hugged himself, elbows tight against his waist, delighted with his own cleverness. "I'm out, an' he said special that I must stay in tonight."

Sevin, that "he" must surely be.

"What is Sevin doing out here?" Maskell asked.

Brian, hand to his mouth, thinking, half turned, looking slantwise through thick baby lashes.

"If he's found out I've gone, Sevin'll be out looking for me," he said slyly. "You won't tell him where I am?"

"I won't tell him. Where does Sevin live when he isn't out looking for you?"

"In the ground," Brian said absently, picking up the towel he had been using and starting to fold it with slow exaggerated care. "Sevin lives with S'lena down under the ground." He set the folded towel neatly alongside the cutlery on the draining board.

Maskell stared at him. Under the ground, he had said in that child's guileless voice that couldn't tell a lie. You could tell by looking at his transparent face that he was incapable of false-hood.

"Whereabouts, under the ground?" Maskell asked.

But their work done, Brian's hands were still.

"I've been sick," he said, the old refrain. "I mustn't get close to anyone 'cause if I do they'll get it too." He looked longingly at the back door.

"Then if you live with Sevin, he must have been sick too."

"Sevin doesn't get sick. Not ever, he doesn't get sick. Nor S'lena." He looked at Maskell. "They wouldn't like it if they found I'd been talking to you."

He had certainly emphasised the "you," as if it wouldn't have mattered if he were caught with anyone else.

Maskell seized on that emphasis. "Why me, Brian? Do they know me?"

Brian thought about that. "No, they don't know you, I think. They just saw you. They both saw you. Through a window. An' they say you saw them too, and it was all my fault." His pale baby eyes brimmed with sudden tears. "Sevin was bad angry with me because they thought you'd seen them."

Out of the mouths of babes and sucklings and mentally deficients . . .

Maskell said: "You mean Sevin and Selena don't want me to see them at all?"

"They don't want no one to see them," said Brian simply.

And he wasn't lying again. Maskell knew, *knew*, that that was one thing he could be sure about. Which meant the charade hadn't been laid on for his benefit. For no one's benefit, come to that. Which made no sense at all. People don't dress up like that to take a midnight stroll on the moors, even if they are on the stage.

He said: "Sevin's a conjurer, isn't he, Brian?"

Brian edging doorwards, stopped, knuckles to his eyes, wiping away the earlier tears. "What's a con—conch—?" He couldn't get the word out.

"A magician. You know." Maskell, frowning slightly, gestured. "On the stage. He makes things vanish, and other things disappear. That's why he wears those special clothes."

The other was clearly intrigued by the picture evoked. "Like in a story? I like stories. Fairies . . . Oh—an' in a pantomime once. Magic. Like that?"

Whatever Sevin was, it seemed he wasn't a stage magician. Otherwise, Brian would at least have known something about it. And yet: "*Sevin can do things other people can't.*"

Brian had finally edged his way to the door. "Don't go," Maskell cried, and sought for an excuse, any excuse, to keep him there. A drink, perhaps . . . "Won't you stay and have a drink with me, Brian? I've got coffee or tea." And a lucky afterthought. "Beer?"

Brian stopped again, his hand on the latch. "I've never had beer. Is it nice?"

More importantly, having done the trick, was there any beer left? When Maskell went towards the cupboards to find out, his visitor moved crabwise away, keeping a respectable distance between them.

There was one can—no, two—left. Maskell held them up. "Shall we share them between us? Let's go to the other room, it's nicer in there." And it was also less easy to escape from.

Brian clasped long white hands together in excitement. "They never let me have beer to drink; oh—never, never, not never."

And was there, Maskell wondered, some special reason why beer had been kept away from him? Perhaps because they were afraid that alcohol might get him worked up, excited. Were mentally deficient people, like ordinary ones, apt to do more talking than usual under the influence. Maskell nodded at the shelves. "Bring a couple of glasses, and let's go have ourselves a party."

He led the way, cans in one hand, oil lamp in the other, Brian tagging excitedly along behind, but still careful to keep his distance. In the lounge he set down the lamp to add its illumination to the one already there, and then stooped to poke the fire. "We may as well make ourselves comfortable." It wasn't all that much warmer here than in the kitchen. "Don't you feel cold, wearing just that shirt?"

"I'm not wearing just a shirt. There's other things." Brian put the tumblers on the table and watched with fascinated gaze while Maskell opened both cans and filled the glasses, then, carrying his own glass, left the other for Brian to pick up in his own good time.

Brian sipped the beer cautiously and made a face, wrinkling his nose in the way of a child with nasty-tasting medicine. "It's not very nice."

"You'll get used to it," Maskell encouraged. "Have another sip." And wondered if this sort of beer was strong enough to have any effect at all.

Brian emptied his glass. And then, eyes hooded, so far forgot himself as to allow Maskell to come close enough to refill it.

Brian sipped at the replenished glass, at the same time rubbing his stomach. "Makes you feel warm down here." And, blinking sleepily, swaying just a little, touched his forehead. "Funny up here too, going round and round, like when I've had my medicine."

Medicine . . . Something Maskell, immediately alarmed, hadn't thought about. And should have; it stood to reason that there was a good chance of someone in Brian's condition having to take medicine of some kind. A sedative—almost certainly a sedative. Some sort of drug. And now alcohol was being added to it. He could have kicked himself for not having considered the very obvious possibility of Brian being on drugs.

"I don't think you should have any more," he said quickly, but wasn't quite fast enough to grasp the tumbler before Brian, a disobedient child, had stepped back out of reach.

"Put your glass on the table, Brian," Maskell said gently.

"Don't want to." A child now, in every sense of the word,

Brian gulped down the contents of his glass before it could be taken away from him. And then, after closing his eyes for a few moments, had trouble replacing the empty glass on the table, opening his fingers when his hand was still inches away, letting it fall with a clatter. "I got to go now," he said, the words ever so slightly slurred.

The damage, if any, was done. Maskell, sorry for what had happened, still saw no reason why he shouldn't try to take advantage of any tongue-loosening that might result.

So: "Is Sevin your father, Brian?"

Brian blinked as if trying to clear his vision. He clutched the leather back of one of the chairs to steady himself. His twin shadows swayed in sympathy across the walls.

"I don't have no father," he said dreamily. "Nor no mother. Nor nobody. Except S'vin an' S'lena."

"What are all of you doing out here, Brian?"

"We're—oh—doin' things. All sorts of things. I've been sick, an' now I'm getting better an' I have to do as I'm told." Brian's voice now was the singsong of a small child repeating a kindergarten litany. "An' I mus' always take my medicine, an' do like Doctor Deakin says, an' not tell no one, never; an' do what Sevin says, an' what S'lena says, an' what George says, an' when I'm—"

At which point Brian closed his eyes, let go of the back of the chair and slid gently to the floor. He was out cold, Maskell found, having for the second time gone through his new eyelid-raising routine. And another second time for the hoisting of an unconscious body onto the settee; if anything, this one heavier than Fairfield had been. Brian exuded a kind of warm yeasty smell that one normally associates with very small babies, Maskell discovered, straightening.

Pillow under tight brown curls, blanket over sawdust-limp body, and that was about all that could be done. And having tucked the blanket in, Maskell went to lean on the mantelpiece and stare down at the now feeble blaze.

Two more names to add to the list. Doctor Deakin, whoever he was. And someone called simply "George." A good, steady, dependable name, George. The sort of name that inspires confidence. If the rest of them were anything to go by, he would probably turn out to have horns and a tail.

So, five people in all, now. And where were they all living? Five people to be fed and watered and provided with sleeping quarters and all the rest.

And what sort of picture could the bits and pieces be made into now? Say Sevin and Selena were father and daughter—impossible to consider them being husband and wife—and if not on the stage, then they ought to be, with names like that and their fancy dresses. Brian was Sevin's adopted son. Not very feasible, that, but the only thing that made sense. Brian had been ill—no doubts on that score—now required peace and quiet, and so his adopted father and sister, rich enough to afford a private doctor, had brought some doctor out here with them to help Brian convalesce. And George? Manservant, maybe. Or perhaps male nurse.

All of which, Maskell felt, was so much wasted time and energy and probably couldn't be farther from the truth. He pulled back his sweater sleeve so that he could see his watch. Half past ten. Later than he'd thought. Time, after standing still, now seemed to be racing. And if he had been hungry earlier, he was famished now.

He took one of the lamps with him to the kitchen, at home now with the dancing of his own sprawling shadow across the high bare walls of the hall. The only sounds were the padding of his rubber soles and the slow ticking of the clock.

He found and broke a small wooden box to get the fire going quickly. Waiting for the flames to take hold, he went to stand by the window, leaning over the sink to stare out into the night. A haze of luminosity showed where the moon was trying to break through the clouds.

The feeling of calmness and self-confidence that filled him now must be unnatural, induced as an aftereffect by whatever had caused the hallucinations. On the other hand, he had never before found himself in a situation like this—he doubted whether many people had—and so it was remotely possible that his reactions owed nothing to artificial aids; it would be nice to think that he was able to cope on his own, using his own previously untapped resources.

From the cupboards he chose cans pretty much at random. The way he was feeling, food was food whatever the labels said. Struggling with the clumsy can opener, whistling softly through his teeth, he broke off suddenly, listening, fancying he had heard a sound. Imagination again . . . But then, busy with his own thoughts, he had temporarily forgotten about Brian. He had probably come round and was on the move again. Leaving the kitchen door open behind him to light the way, Maskell hurried across the hall and into the lounge. Brian still lay on the settee, but asleep now rather than unconscious, if his changed position and easier breathing were any guide.

Straightening, Maskell looked through the open door into the darkness of the adjoining room. Whatever had caused the sound, it had come from in there. And here he was, standing clear in the lamplight, visible for miles around, just as Fairfield must have been before he bought it. He moved to the lamp and turned the wick down until the flame flickered and died, leaving the lounge now also in darkness.

Two more silent paces took him to the wall alongside the doorway. His back pressed against it, head cocked, he listened intently, straining to catch the slightest sound. When he could pick up nothing, he edged sideways until he was able to peer round the corner. And now there was a sound in the darkness, like the soft creaming of surf on a beach, defying recognition for a moment, then suddenly becoming breathing other than his own. And for him to be able to hear that meant that the source must be only inches away.

At which point the clouds parted and moonlight came flooding through uncurtained windows, silhouetting the person—it could have been either a man or a woman—who stood there, half crouching, it seemed, in what was certainly a threatening attitude. And because of that immediate impression of an animal crouched to spring, Maskell—this the first time in his life he had ever attempted to physically harm another human being—blundered forward, clenched fists swinging wildly, trusting to luck rather than judgement that they would do something useful. One came up against something hard—a chin, he hoped. The force of the other was lost in bunched-up cloth. There was a blind, undignified scuffle, a grunt, a muttered exclamation, one vague retaliatory blow that glanced off the side of his head, and it was over, the intruder turning to blunder back towards the french windows, still only a shapeless form, leaving behind the faint but distinct smell of some kind of antiseptic.

Maskell, triumphant, breathing heavily, was ready to follow, had in fact started in pursuit, when another sound, this time coming from behind, brought him to a halt, head turned to listen. The front door being opened; no doubt about that, a sound he had become very accustomed to. And now voices, men's voices, too indistinct as yet to be identifiable, but one with a familiar ring to it that smacked of Fairfield's throaty tones.

Was indeed Fairfield's voice. Maskell, swiftly and silently back across the lounge to perform his back-pressing manoeuvre against another wall alongside another door, peered cautiously round another corner to see Fairfield, clear in the moonlight, standing by the open front door, seeming by his gestures—his actual words inaudible—to be inviting the other man, as yet out of sight, into the house. And, waiting to see the outcome of that invitation, Maskell found something odd about Fairfield, something not right about his appearance, but was unable to put his finger on it, had no time to think about it, for now Fairfield's companion came inside to join him; the man in the black cloak, as Maskell had felt almost sure it must be; Sevin, with Fairfield, complicity finally out into the open, talking to each other in the friendliest way possible, as if they had known each other all their lives.

And suddenly Maskell saw how all this was part of a concerted effort, the thing finally coming to a head, a moving in on him from all sides: one through the french windows, two through the front door—there would be another at the back door, others at various vantage points. He turned to gaze into the darkness in the direction of the far room. Having launched his attack first and put one intruder to flight, there was a chance he might be able to take advantage of the gap before they were able to refill it. He had no intention of staying put and allowing himself to be taken. He went quickly back across the room, avoiding chairs and settee by memory and touch, into the adjoining room—easier to see in there with more and larger windows to let in the moonlight—empty, the french windows unguarded—through the ready open centre one, along the moonlit terrace, half crouching, running on the balls of his feet; a pause when he reached the corner and peered round, then, all clear, down the side of the house to the drive, and still nobody to challenge him, so along the drive to the road, there to turn in the direction of the deserted village, the only way he could go if he were to stand any chance of throwing off the almost certain pursuit.

He kept running until laboured breathing combined with a knife pain in his side to force him down to, first, a jog trot, then a walk. And quite suddenly, without having to think about it, it came to him what had been strange about Fairfield, what had been wrong—terribly, frighteningly wrong . . .

Fairfield had stood there full in the moonlight from the open door, every last detail of that side of his face and head visible to Maskell, sharp and clear. The same side of his head that had received the blow, that should have carried a large patch of purple bruise and a ragged line of dried blood where the flesh had been broken.

But instead had carried nothing, the flesh whole again, no sign of either bruise or scar or blood. It was as if a hand had moved across that side of his head, wiping away every trace of the blow.

ELEVEN

A haze had come to obscure the moon, not thick enough to completely cut off its light, enough filtering through for Maskell to see the road and, more importantly, the crumbling verges. There were places, he remembered from his daylight walks this way, where black marsh came dangerously close to the far from clearly defined verges.

He stopped when some distance away from the house, turning back to see if there was any sign of the expected pursuit. That they would follow him, he felt very certain. They wouldn't give up just because he had been lucky enough to slip through the net. It seemed that having disposed of the softening-up preliminaries they were now getting down to the job of—of what? He just didn't know. This was a development he had never expected, so certain in his own mind that the campaign against him, against his sanity, rather, would never become a physical affair. As he saw it, by bringing it out into the open the way they had, they had undone all their carefully planned psychological touches, weakened the whole campaign. Anyone can cope with a fist; not many can take ghostly voices and telephone bells in their stride. And that last trick of theirs . . . Fairfield's return to normal, and God, how had they managed that? How had they been able to heal open flesh and smooth away angry bruising in little over an hour?

Impossible, but it had happened. He had seen with his own eyes under conditions that would seem to have precluded trickery. And he hadn't made a mistake; the side of Fairfield's head that he had seen so clearly in the moonlight was the same side that had received the impact of the blow. In any case, when Fairfield had turned, for some reason, to look in the direction of the kitchen, the other side of his head had come into view, and that too had been clean and whole.

How they had done the impossible, Maskell for the life of him couldn't even start to imagine. And puzzling over it, trying to find some sort of answer, thinking in terms of stage illusion, remembered something Brian had said. *"Sevin can do things other people can't."* A remark that was the product of a deranged child's mind, nothing more, not to be taken seriously, certainly not to be thought of in the context of open wounds being miraculously fleshed over.

His breathing easy again, the pain gone from his side, Maskell resumed walking. His original dash from the house seemed to have brought him more than halfway to the village. To the deserted village—no food, no bed, no warmth, no real shelter, only a roof over his head if it should happen to rain. Which right now seemed a distinct possibility, the moon, still behind its gauzy nimbus screen, threatened by darkly surging clouds. He quickened his pace, hoping to reach the cottages—or the pub; that would be his best bet—before darkness came.

It came, the pale moonlight wiped away as if by a giant hand, just as he reached the grassy triangle at the heart of the village. But the night still provided enough light to enable him to find his way to The Highlander without too much difficulty. He stumbled over the step into the pitch-black of the room that must once have been the bar. The smell of cooking still lingered in the small rear room. It brought to mind the other smell he had encountered recently, that of antiseptics that had clung to the person with whom he had fought—fought; that was a laugh —back at the house. Not so much antiseptics in particular, thinking back, but a kind of general chemist's shop smell. Or that of a doctor's surgery. Surely not Brian's Doctor Deakin, his opponent in that inglorious tussle?

He went back into the long front room, feeling his way along the wall in the direction of the fireplace, remembering from the last time he was here—here they were now—his fingers found the curved wooden screen of one of the inglenook seats. They may have ripped the pews out of the church and carted them away, but at least they had left these, probably because they were built into the wall, part of the actual structure.

Smooth and friendly warm to the touch; indentations worn into the wood—like hollowed stone steps in a monastery—by centuries of rural backsides and shoulders. Maskell leaned back, legs stretched out in the darkness, as comfortable as one could hope to be under these conditions.

Under these conditions . . . squatting miserably in a deserted pub in a deserted village in the middle of the night. Lonely, hungry as hell, tired to death and bloody fed up. A wallow of self-pity became swamped in a surge of rage. Who the hell did they think they were, this gang of hoodlums, comic-characters and halfwits. Chasing after him like he was some kind of wild animal. Forced to cower in the darkness like this. He, Boyd Maskell of Saturn . . .

Against which self-pomposity the anger broke, the spasm passed and Maskell smiled wryly into the darkness. Working up a fury like that might be good for the circulation and stir up the adrenal glands, but was otherwise no use at all. Far better use his energies figuring out some way to get out of this unholy— and by God, "unholy" was the right word—out of this unholy mess and back to civilisation in one piece.

And would he have stayed in one piece if they had nabbed him back there at the house? What did they want with him? Perhaps the contents of one of the briefcases he had had to leave behind. No use on their own, those contents. He leaned sideways so that he could feel his hip pocket and reassure himself that the papers there were still safe. Much more likely it was those they were after. But nobody apart from himself knew of their existence. Except possibly Fairfield, who must surely have put two and two together and added it to that partial bluff about ten million sterling. So Fairfield knew, which meant so now did the rest of them, which obviously explained the change in tactics. The original scheme to make a fortune by ousting him from his job had been switched to the far easier and juicier plum of making an even larger fortune by getting their hands on the code. No time to waste, so out into the open. But having got hold of the code, they would have to keep him out of circulation while they made use of it. Weeks at the very least; months if they were out to exploit it to the full. And during all that time his absence would have to be accounted for in such a way as not to arouse suspicion. A man can't just disappear without questions being asked. But a man can have an accident, a very bad accident, even a fatal one, without the faintest breath of suspicion. Which meant that if he were anywhere near the mark with that train of thought, once they had both briefcase and papers, his life might not be worth a brass nickel.

Taking the papers from his pocket, Maskell leaned forward, fumbling in the darkness for the chimney breast, then reaching underneath, using his fingers to explore the rough brickwork. A gap into which his fingers slipped was wide enough to take the papers folded into a narrow oblong. They went easily, perhaps an inch protruding. And now, having found a hiding place for them, his next move must be to put distance between him and it so that if he were caught, there would be nothing to connect him with the place.

A pity, he thought, back on his feet again, to have to leave the quite comfortable inglenook. But in any event, he had never intended spending the night here. If they thought he had fled from the house for good, they were wrong. He was going back, and if any of them were still there, then—some of Fairfield's language having rubbed off on him—sod the bastards. It was high time he did some hitting back. Been far too one-sided so far; his first and only attempt at a rough and tumble being pretty hopeless. Next time, remembering how the heavy kitchen poker had felt, he'd be more scientific in approach. And how much he'd give for a good stiff drink right now.

He groped his way to the door; opened it cautiously. There was just enough light for him to see the signpost on the grass triangle, a stage setting with ghost-white cottages and the dim outline of the solid-square church tower for backdrop. Nothing moved; the silence was like a pall. On a night like this the slightest sound would travel. He tried to recall what sort of shoes Fairfield had worn. Rubber-soled, he fancied, unable to hear footsteps in his mind.

But if they had taken off after him right away, then instead of yet having to come down the road, they might already be here, waiting and watching, knowing full well he must be in one of the empty buildings, that there was simply no place else to go. And in their shoes, where would he wait and watch? Maskell's gaze moved back to the church tower. From up there, as he well knew, almost the whole of the village was in sight. By daylight, that was. He narrowed his eyes up at the sky. By the way the clouds now seemed to be breaking, it was going to be well nigh as bright as daylight within a very few minutes. And if one of them was up there, spotting, while the rest combed the place, then the moment he broke cover his goose was as good as cooked.

He was halfway across the road before he realised he was on the move, some buried animal instinct—or boyhood memories of cowboys and Indians?—telling him to crouch, to cross the open at its narrowest point, to make for the shadow of the opposite cottages; not to pause there, but to cross again, this time to the deeper shadows of the church itself. His back hard against the rough wall, he strained to listen above the thudding of his heart. If there had been a spotter up there, and he had caught the movement, then he hadn't sounded the alarm. If that was it, and he was trying to box clever, then two could play at that game.

The church door was closed. It had been closed this afternoon when he and Fairfield had come exploring, but he had the feeling he had left it open behind him in his anxiety over Fairfield's vanishing act. No matter; there was bound to be another way in—the sort of private door the vicar and the choir and the rest of them used. Maskell started working his way along the front of the church away from the porch. The moon broke through momentarily as he reached the corner, was swept away as he started down the side, now having to keep away from the wall to avoid the buttresses, ploughing through tall grass. An unexpected barrier brought him to a jarring stop. Iron railings, he discovered, the spike-topped uprights badly corroded, some of them rusted completely through. He wrenched one away and was working on a second, to make a gap wide enough to wriggle through, when the moonlight flooded again to show him a gate, the hinges rusty like the rest, but still functional, opening with only a faint grating sound. He balanced the detached length of iron in his hand, testing the feel. It lacked the moulded grip and balance of the poker, but would serve the purpose he had in mind.

A crazy path of uneven stone slabs led from the gate through the coarse grass and time-tilted headstones of the churchyard. Grey granite, by their look, most of the stones, but with here and there the ghost-shape of a white marble cross. A strand of briar reached from nowhere to rake across his cheek. Others snagged at the stuff of his sweater. Swearing under his breath, he worked himself free. Thankfully, the moon had found itself a clear stretch of sky; not daylight by any means, but still bright enough for him to see where he was going—and be seen himself, come to that. He drew closer into the shadows, working his way from one buttress to the next and reaching the end of the wall without coming upon the expected door.

He edged carefully round the corner into an extension of the wilderness of bramble and grass and carved stone. And here, with the path passing between it and the rear of the church, was another building, a toy structure, a miniature marble temple gleaming in the moonlight. A folly of some kind, Maskell thought first, not expecting to find a family mausolem in the tiny churchyard of a rural church. But a mausoleum it was, with the name carved over the pillared portico in classic Roman letters—MALVEN—just that, nothing more. A name he knew from somewhere but couldn't place, only certain that he had come across it very recently; then suddenly remembered that that was the name of the house. Then, had the people who had once lived there been named Malven, and grandiosely called the house after themselves? Or had they thought it marked good breeding and dignity to call the place of their dead by the same simple name as their living?

Either way, there it was, completely out of place in this lonely moorland setting, much more at home in the fanciful, colourful surroundings of an Italian Grand Cemetery. The heavy outer gate of black metal was unfastened, Maskell noticed with some surprise, and open a few inches. If one had a mind to it, one would merely have to stretch out a hand to push it wide open, climb down three stone steps, open the inner gilded gates and then enter the tomb itself. But there was no need to actually enter the place to see what it contained. Curiosity, nothing more, impelled Maskell to climb down the steps and put his face against the cold gilded bars. Moonlight flooded in from behind and through the two narrow grilled windows set high in the bare walls of the tomb to fill the dusty, timeless interior with a cold radiance that reached into every corner, so that it was possible to clearly see the two stone shelves, one on either side of the tomb, and on them the small stone cradles upon which coffins had once rested, the shapes of those coffins outlined by the thick layer of collected dust. And underneath each shelf hollows had been chiselled out of the solid stone of the floor, two coffin-shaped hollows, and those also empty now but for the tracery of dust that showed plainly where the coffins themselves had once been. Once four people named Malven had lain here. Now they were gone. For some reason their coffins had been raised from what should have been their last resting place, carried up the stone steps, loaded onto some sort of conveyance and carried away. And why should anyone want to empty a tomb of its occupants? Maskell shivered a little, backed up the three leaf-littered steps and resumed his search.

A few minutes later it had become apparent there was no other door into the church, that there was consequently to be no sneaking up behind anyone who happened to be lurking in its dim interior. He felt a certain sense of relief. Now he came to think, the idea hadn't been all that clever. The people he was up against here weren't the sort to leave their rear unprotected. He had temporarily forgotten another axiom of High Finance. Never underestimate your opponent. He resumed his way back now towards the road.

And then, almost at the corner, the problem of what his next move should be was taken care of for him. It was the sudden raking flash of white light that drew his attention to the grass triangle. A torch, by its concentrated beam, and surely no need for it to be switched on with everywhere bathed in moonlight. Fairfield, recognisable by his long face, shock of black hair and chunky sweater, had seated himself on the stone bench and was leaning back at his ease, the cheeky bastard, looking up and listening to what his companion was saying. Sevin—Maskell had made up his mind that Brian's Sevin must be the man in the black cloak—was pointing along the road that led to the house, a dramatic gesture, his cloak thrown grandly back, its scarlet lining gleaming. The torch was in his other gloved hand, pointing down now, lighting a distorted oval of bright green grass.

Maskell drew hurriedly back into the shadow of the corner buttress, only just realising that his sweater, unlike Fairfield's grey one, wasn't the best of colours for this sort of caper, that its whiteness must stand out like a beacon. He had a sudden mental image of the elderly gentleman assistant in Harrod's and his courteous: "Always a serviceable colour, white, sir. Goes well with everything; suitable for every open-air occasion." Except perhaps churchyard shadows on hunted moonlit nights, Maskell thought wryly, and peered cautiously round the stone corner. Sevin was now using the torch to point in the direction of the road that led past the pub, while Fairfield, luxuriating on his bench, not a care in the world to look at him, seemed to be agreeing with whatever the other was saying.

It seemed to Maskell that they were discussing in which direction to start searching for him. Or perhaps not, for now Fairfield was up on his feet, hands blithely on hips, and the two of them were walking side by side—an incongruous couple—along the road Sevin had indicated, leading past The Highlander and ending at the ruined farm. And passing en route, Maskell now recalled, the derelict cottage towards which Sevin had made his way earlier that afternoon, and which Fairfield later said he had explored and found empty. It could be there was more to that particular cottage than met the eye.

The two men disappeared round a bend in the road. Gripping his makeshift cudgel, Maskell ran lightly, bent double, across the open space towards the green, across that pointed stretch of grass and into the far road, slowing to a walk as he approached

the bend, rounding it warily, close in to the low stone wall front-
ing those particular cottages. And as he came round to the other
side, so darkness came down like Sevin's black cloak, swollen to
earth-covering proportions, being trailed across the landscape.
Pitch-black now, the night, by contrast. But there ahead was the
torch, swinging from one side of the road to the other like a
miniature searchlight beam, being carried carelessly, swivelling
to and fro with the natural movement of the carrying hand.
Abruptly the swinging stopped and the beam swung round, the
torch held firmly now, to point at right angles away from the
road. And where that had happened, Maskell quietly exulted,
would be just outside the ruined cottage. He quickened his pace,
watching the beam and the pair of shadowy figures in its wake
slide behind a bush, then flick out of existence. They had gone
inside the cottage, Maskell interpreted, and then, the destination
confirmed, took his time over his own approach, having no intention of walking into anything remotely resembling a trap.

The front of the cottage loomed up, an oblong white face with
dark windows for eyes and dark door for mouth; gaping windows
and crumbling doorway, with nothing but emptiness behind
them. Nobody in the cottage at all. He emerged from the back
door—this would be the same door, he supposed, where the
stone had caught Fairfield's shoulder; if that was really what had
happened—and there, not far ahead, the light danced like a will-
o'-the-wisp over the moorland. They had not gone into the cottage, but along its side, perhaps following a path . . .

There was a path; cinders by the feel, to start with, but becoming packed earth almost immediately. His quarry—it was good to
think of them as that—couldn't be even as far in front as he had
first thought; there hadn't been time for them to cover any distance. They were in single file, which suggested that where they
were walking now the path had become more narrow. And they
were certainly walking more slowly and, by their movements,
with some caution. And seeing that, remembering the treacherous quality of the moorland, brought Maskell to a halt. Without the aid of a light and with no local knowledge at all, it
seemed foolhardy to carry on. But if it was safe enough for the

two in front—surely not local people in any way—then it was worth the risk to find out where they were making for.

He started off again. So far, moving in a more or less straight line, they had been easy and safe enough to follow from the distance. All he had to do was keep an eye on them, and if they did change direction, make a note of the spot and then do the same himself. Then, intent upon the dancing torchlight, he put one foot down a little to the side onto something jellylike that gave alarmingly under his weight. Recovering, he started using his iron rail as a probe to test the width of the path whenever its solidness seemed in doubt. Moonlight broke through for a moment, and he dropped instinctively to one knee, crouching low in case either of the two ahead should happen to turn round. The light faded, and he resumed walking, more quickly now, trying to lessen the distance between.

His gaze was actually on the torch beam when it flicked out of existence. But now he was near enough to be able to make out Sevin and Fairfield without its aid, two shapes dimly visible against the faint glow of the skyline. And in that same moment the shapes themselves vanished, seeming to his narrowed straining gaze to concertina down on themselves like deflated rubber figures—one moment there, the next, collapsed and gone. A hollow in the ground, he thought; they will reappear in a second. But the horizon frieze remained empty, and when he reached the place where it had happened, he found the path level, no hint of even the slightest depression. Grass grew rough and tall on one side, and on the other an outcropping of tumbled rock was topped with skeletal bushes. Water glinted steely cold. Reeds rustled, papyrus-brittle, with the scuffling of some small creature. Otherwise the night was silent. It was as if the ground had opened to swallow up the two men.

And, born of that far from original notion, something Brian in his childlike meanderings had said came to mind. *"They live down under the ground,"* talking of Sevin and Selena. Which had been his way of saying they lived in a basement or cellar or somewhere similar. Must have been. There was no other sensible interpretation.

His makeshift weapon clutched tightly, Maskell slowly re-volved, looking in every direction. Ahead, the path came to a dead end in a patch of tall reeds. Behind, it reached back in an almost straight line to the now invisible village. And all round, nothing as far as his eye could reach but empty moorland.

Another thought occurred to him. Those two, they hadn't known he was following them, he was sure of that. What he had just seen happen had happened in the ordinary course of events—ordinary only so far as these people were con-cerned—and had not been something laid on specially for his benefit, not an effect rigged to mystify and frighten. Something unusual was going on here that had nothing at all to do with him.

But whatever that something was, he was fast being drawn into it.

░░░ TWELVE ░░░

Maskell, having learned to treat the ground that verged the path with great respect, trod slowly and carefully on his way back to the village, probing when in doubt, not hurrying, and that despite a great urge to be in out of the open and safe in the psychological sanctuary of the empty cottages. And reaching that particular cottage that marked the start of the path, he spent an uncomfortable few minutes wrestling with a bout of nausea, not actually vomiting, but feeling the need to. The result of a sudden relaxing of tension, he thought at first, the spasm easing. But then put it down to the fact that it was for him, a very regular eater, a long time since any food had passed his lips. And that was what the fleshpots of the West End did for you. His next job must be to get something inside that sick-making emptiness.

But first he looked back across the dark expanse of moor. They had gone somewhere, Sevin and Fairfield; into Brian's under-the-ground, because there was simply no other answer. If it had been daylight he would have stopped out there and searched until he had found the place. But why should anyone in their right mind have gone to the trouble of excavating and fitting out some sort of subterranean hideaway when there was a village full of empty cottages just aching to be made use of? Another imponderable, if that was the word, to add to the rest. One day he'd look back and laugh at all this. Laugh . . . At this moment all he felt like doing was folding his head in his arms and wishing himself into oblivion. His earlier confidence had evaporated. But who the hell anyway could feel cocky without any food inside them? The remedy to that situation lay in the house. Maskell, walking back through the village, wished there was an alternative way of approaching the house other than by the very open and exposed road.

At least the continuing darkness afforded some kind of cover.

If any of them were still in the house, and watching, he should be able to get reasonably close without being spotted. So long as the darkness lasted . . . By the look of the sky—a melange of all kinds of cloud formation—nothing could be guaranteed. If the moon did break through at the crucial moment it would be a case of making a dash for it and hoping for the best.

He kept well to the centre of the road, mindful of the crumbling verges. He had wondered before about the shocking state of its surface; he wondered again now, his feet slipping and sliding over patches of churned-up gravel. It was almost as if pickaxes had been systematically used in a deliberate attempt to destroy the surface. Normal traffic could never have created this sort of havoc.

The front of the house, when it loomed up, was in darkness. He remembered turning out the oil lamp in the lounge—that would be that first group of three windows to the right of the front door—but he felt sure he had left the lamp in the kitchen burning. If there were watchers in there, some would be covering the back, and they would have turned out the kitchen lamp to be able to see out of the window.

But that was working on the original assumption that he was their target. The assumption of egoism. I am the great Boyd Maskell. Whatever is going on, because of who I am, I am bound to be at its centre. That was the way he had had things figured from the start. Now it seemed he could have figured wrong. All the same, Maskell told himself, just to be on the safe side it would be best to continue thinking along the same lines until there was more proof to the contrary than a demonstration of the unusual that didn't appear to have been staged for his benefit.

He trod lightly on the gravel of the drive, keeping close in to the line of bushes so that their shadow would mask his outline if the moon did come out, cutting across a strip of earth that may at one time have been a flowerbed to reach the side of the house. He wondered, making his way towards the rear terrace, if Brian was still sleeping it off on the settee. He didn't think it very likely.

Edging carefully round the corner, he could tell by the light splashed across the terrace that the lamp in the kitchen was still burning. Taking no chances, he crouched below the window, raising his head slowly to peer into the room. Empty. It was just as he had left it, the table littered with the cans he had put out for his interrupted meal, some of them open. Opening the back door, careful not to rattle the latch, he tiptoed silently over to the other door to go out into the hall and stand and listen. If anyone else was in the hosue, they were keeping remarkably quiet. Lamp in one hand, iron rail poised in the other, he set out to make sure.

As he had anticipated, the settee in the lounge was empty. The blanket and pillow, roughly bundled to one side, were both cold to the touch. Gone some time, then. But under his own steam, he wondered with some anxiety, or had he been carried? The former, he hoped fervently, still feeling guilty. Brian was the very last person he would intentionally try to harm.

There was a smell, he noticed. Not clinging to the blanket, but just generally in the air. It seemed he had spent much of his time of late in discovering smells of one kind or another and putting names to them. No trouble with this one. Tobacco smoke. Cigarettes, if he was any judge. Not Fairfield—he hadn't smoked in all the time they had been together. He didn't think Brian was a likely candidate. He had seen Sevin twice—no, three times—and on none of those occasions had he been smoking. It seemed probable that the antiseptic-redolent intruder had been the offender. Not that it mattered much, and he was surprised that he had let himself waste time thinking about it. It was almost as if his mind, working on its own volition, had run through the list of names for its own information and assessment.

Lamp held high, Maskell continued on his rounds. There was no one else in the house; no sign, apart from the smell of tobacco smoke, of anyone having been there. In the kitchen he piled paper and broken wood in the grate, set a match to it, ran enough water for one cup of coffee into a saucepan, put the pan on the blaze and then, not bothering about the niceties of sitting down or using a plate, started spooning the contents of one of the cans into his mouth. He had never realised cold pork and beans could be so delicious.

The man in the shadow of the copse that bordered the drive in front of the house took out a packet of cigarettes and, about to put one between his lips, changed his mind. He could have used a fag; there would have been no chance worth mentioning of its glowing tip being seen from the house, but if the doc was to show up, as he was likely to at any moment, then there would be Old Harry to pay. So George Blake, known as "Blakey" to his fellow workers in a certain doubtful private mental sanitarium, returned his cigarettes regretfully to his pocket and leaned against a neighbouring tree. He had earlier watched Maskell's return and then followed the drift of the lamp as it had passed from one room to the next, and he had smiled a little to himself imagining how the man conducting that search was likely to be feeling. In his opinion—confused, to say the least. And that was the opinion of someone who, in his own way, was something of an expert on the workings of the human mind. And now, the search concluded, the confused searcher would, hopefully, be having something to eat and drink. Blake smiled his complacent little smile.

Leaves rustled; not loud enough, he thought, for there to be anyone there, but just in case it was the doctor, he gave a low whistle to show where he was. When there was no response he turned back to resume watch on the house. He wondered, with no great interest, who the man calling himself "Dr. Deakin" really was. Hardly a medical type, he felt. He had already discovered that his employer wasn't accustomed to being addressed as "Doctor," that he didn't always answer first time to the title.

But who and what he really was was no concern of his just so long as the lolly continued to flow his way, with the firm promise of a grand-slam bonus that should set him up for life if things worked out right.

Rustling leaves again disturbed his reverie. This time, not the breeze, but someone whose eyes, used to the dark, hadn't needed a whistle to guide him.

"Well?" Dr. Deakin asked softly, looking at the dark shape of the house.

"He's in there now." Blake pushed himself away from his tree. "Came sneaking back about fifteen minutes ago, went through all the rooms—making sure he was alone again, I suppose—and now, with some luck—he should be in the kitchen, getting himself a bite to eat. I hope so, anyway." He used his half-smile again. "Banking on it, you could say."

"I see. What did you use this time?"

Blake grimaced at the emphasis on the last two words. "Nothing so elaborate. The good old standby. Knockout drops, to the trade. Old-fashioned, but effective. Chloral hydrate. No nutterward should be without them." It was too dark to see his companion's heavy frown. "Fixed three tins of assorted solids and a can of milk. Bound to have a go at at least one of them. My money's on the milk. Should go out like a light in ten minutes."

"No obvious aftereffects," Deakin said. At least he had that much medical knowledge. "Pentothal would have been better, though." He peered down at the luminous dial of his watch. "Ten minutes . . ."

"I went through the place while he was away," Blake offered conversationally. "Nothing much. Tell you what I did come across. You'd never guess. Although"—with second thoughts—"maybe you would. Tape recorder rigged up with time switch. You want to know what was on the tape?"

"No," Deakin said shortly.

"I thought you might know." Blake sounded disappointed. "Your idea?"

Deakin looked at his watch again. "He should have had long enough by now."

"Give it another five minutes." Blake looked up at the sky. "Bit of all sorts up there tonight. Rain before morning, I'd say." His gaze returned to the dark shape of the house. "You reckon it'll work out all right, Doc?" He jerked his head. "Abacus?"

"I think so," said the man who had only recently taken to calling himself "Doctor."

The cold pork and beans had been good; the white greasy sausages not so good. But the rice pudding, something Maskell had often wondered about when advertised on television, had turned out to be surprisingly delicious. To round off quite a satisfying meal, the water for the instant coffee had boiled at just the right moment. He added milk and then left it to cool while he tipped the empty cans into the cardboard box in the corner. He yawned widely—so hugely, in fact, that he had to grip hold of the side of the table to prevent being swayed off his feet. With repletion had come tiredness. Bed, as soon as he'd had the coffee, and the best place for sleeping would be up in the bedroom where there was only the one door to be barricaded against possible intruders.

He took the still-too-hot-to-drink coffee with him on his yawning, far from steady way up the stairs. And along the landing, with one hand filled with coffee cup and the other with the lamp, unable to use either to steady himself, he staggered back and forth from one wall to the other.

And in the bedroom—barely able to keep his eyes open—having managed with some difficulty to set the lamp safely down on the dressing table, when he tried to do the same with the cup he missed his aim and then let go of it in midair. He stood swaying, not able to see clearly, blinking down at the steaming pool on the floor, until the floor started to come up slowly to meet him.

"Had himself a rare old tuck-in," Blake said in the kitchen, the narrow beam of his small pocket torch sweeping over the table, empty now save for one solitary can. "You can tell he's not used to this sort of thing. Cut off the whole top of the can of milk instead of just puncturing it. Made it easier for me to put the dope in. Put the biggest dose in the milk; seemed the surest." The circle of light dwindled and brightened as he came nearer. "Used a good half of it," he observed with satisfaction. "Let's go see how far he got before flaking out."

"You're sure about the other one this time?" Deakin asked in the hall.

"No more trouble from him." Blake used his torch to show the look of confidence on his face. "I guarantee it."

From the lounge doorway, he swung the beam round the empty room. "Figured he might have made for the settee. Bed, then?" The beam, climbing the stairs, found a small damp patch. "Upstairs it is. See where he slopped coffee on his way up?"

At the top of the stairs he switched off the torch, able to see now by the light that spilled from an open bedroom door. "So he managed to make it to his bed." And inside: "Almost, anyway. Looks like he came a fair old cropper. Don't think he's knocked any pieces off himself, though."

But Deakin was more concerned about other things than whether or not Maskell had hurt himself in falling. Straightening up from bending over the unconscious man, his face was black. It was an expression that Blake had come to learn was best treated with respect. He said soberly: "You'll do better if we get him up off the floor."

"Take his head," the other said shortly. They lifted Maskell onto the bed. He was breathing noisily, his mouth open, his hands flopping limply at his sides. The doctor bent over him again while Blake watched with interest. They exchanged very few words. After a while Deakin straightened again, his face still dark, thoughtfully rubbing the side of his long slanting jaw. He consulted his watch. "Almost one o'clock." He stepped aside to regard the broken cup and coffee-stained floorboards. "There's no way of telling how much he got inside him before he passed out."

"I don't reckon it matters all that much," Blake said. "He must have soaked up more than enough from the other three cans to keep him quiet for eight hours at least. And anyway, he must have been well nigh out on his feet to start with. He's not going to get up and go anywhere for quite some time. He'll be here waiting if you want him again."

He paused before adding significantly: "And likely you will. It's little enough to go on." He got an idea. "We could use Pudsey's help, yes? Spin him some yarn or other. And his old woman."

The idea held no appeal for Deakin. "And what sort of yarn could you spin that he would believe?" he asked coldly. "Just because he is what he is doesn't mean he lacks intelligence. He's like you—doing what he is doing for the sake of money."

Blake grinned faintly. "Aren't we all. All right, you're the gaffer. Your way it is." He leaned forward to lightly pat Maskell's cheek. "Nighty-night, sonny-boy. Sleep tight."

The reason the four men, two of them leaving the house, the other pair approaching it, didn't run into each other was because while Dr. Deakin and George Blake were leaving by the front door, Fairfield and an individual going by the name of Albert Pudsey were approaching by a footpath over the moorland that came out quite close to the terrace, thus making one of the french windows the most convenient way of entering the place.

Pudsey, in his midfifties, solid-featured, stocky in build and slow of movement, with a great air of middle-class genteel respectability produced by a combination of his manner of speech, neat grey hair, blue serge suit, white flannel shirt and narrow red tie, switched on his torch as he entered the house. Having of late spent much of his normal sleeping time out of bed, he would much rather have been in that bed now instead of—at one o'clock in the morning—traipsing—his own word—over the moors to have a chat with a gent who might not even be in the house now they had got here. He had allowed Fairfield to persuade him that the gent in question would be sure to be back in the house by now, there being no other place for him to go. And he had further allowed himself to be persuaded of the urgency of the thing. But while letting himself be so persuaded, he had a feeling that there was much more to Fairfield's concern than met the eye. He could quite see why the gent—a Mr. Maxwell—should have become disturbed by some of the things that had been happening. But he found it hard to believe that those happenings should have brought him, as Fairfield had said, to the verge of complete breakdown.

"Getting it sorted out for him could have waited till tomorrow," Fairfield had said as they made their way across the moorland, "but by then the damage might have been done. You don't know the state he's in. And it's your little lot that are responsible. Well"—he qualified that—"mostly responsible. That's if Brian really did have nothing to do with that first dosing."

"In all his life," Pudsey said with great dignity, "Brian never has at any time told me a falsehood."

"Well, anyway, what with one thing after another, Mr. Maskell's got himself into a fine old state. Believe me, Albert, he's not far off cracking up. I know the signs. Another night on his tod in that bloody place and he'll likely be over the brink. He's got to be put in the picture before it's too late. But he won't listen to me—I'm positive of that. It's got to come from the horse's mouth, don't you see, Albert? Then maybe he'll listen. You wouldn't want to have a raving lunatic on your conscience, would you?"

Pudsey said stolidly: "I can quite see as how I 'ave to accept some of the responsibility for the way he is, if he's as bad as you say he is, but only some of it. I'm not asking questions about you, Mr. Fairfield. I'm taking your word as 'ow you've just dropped accidentally into all this. Well, per'aps you 'as, and per'aps you hasn't, but for someone as is saying that he's only just met this Mr. Max—Maskell, then it seems to me that you're going to a very great deal of trouble to help a stranger. If he is back in the house again now—"

"He will be," Fairfield assured him. "You'll see. He knows he can barricade himself in one of the rooms, which is something he can't do anywhere else. I know just how his mind'll work. He'll be up in one of the bedrooms with furniture piled behind the door, and I don't think he'll even then risk closing his eyes."

And because he was so sure that that was how it would be, Fairfield, upon entering the house, took the torch, without asking, from Pudsey's fingers and led the way directly to the hall and up the stairs. He was startled to see the flood of light from the open bedroom door.

"He's asleep," he said in an aggrieved voice from the doorway. "Like a bleeding baby." Then he saw the pieces of the broken cup and the still damp patch on the floorboards. Watched by Pudsey, hovering unhappily on the threshold, he rose from examining the coffee stain to turn his attention back to the man on the bed. Maskell lay like a rag doll that had been dropped there from a height—fully dressed, head lolling to one side, mouth wide, legs at awkward angles, one arm twisted in an unnatural position across his chest.

"Well, I'm buggered," Fairfield growled softly. "He's not asleep. He's out again. Come and see for yourself, man. It's been done on him again."

"Are you sure?" Pudsey, even more unhappy, came to stand at the other side of the bed. "I don't know—"

"Oh, for God's sake . . . He never got on the bed by himself, not to end up in that position. He was put there. You can see what happened. The stuff must have been in that cup. He must have made the coffee downstairs and brought it up here with him to have in bed. He takes a sip or two, goes to do something else, comes back, picks up the cup again, and then, wham, it hits him and he goes down like a log, smashing the cup. And then somebody comes along and picks him up and drops him on the bed. Not all that long ago, either—the floor's still pretty wet."

"It wasn't Brian," Pudsey said, determined to make that clear from the start. "We had to keep him in tonight. Clara's been with him all the time. It wasn't Brian this time." And having said all that, shook his head, his solid features puckered with puzzlement. "But who else could it be? Who would want to do it to him? It doesn't make sense."

"I don't know about the who," Fairfield mused. "I might have a guess at the why." He bent over Maskell, raising him with an effort just enough for him to be able to feel first in his hip pocket, then, lowering him again, the other two. Between them, all they contained were a handkerchief and some loose change.

Straightening, he met Pudsey's look of query. "There were some papers he had," he explained. "He seemed to think they were very important. It's a long story—something to do with finance. The last time I saw him he had them in one of his pockets. Now they've gone."

"Somebody took them," Pudsey said bleakly.

"Or else he found another hiding place for them." Fairfield shook his head at his own suggestion. "I don't think he'd have done that, though."

"Who could it be, then?" Pudsey's square face was a mask of misery that seemed out of proportion to what was happening. "If something's been stolen, then it's got to be one of us, because there's nobody else out here but just us few. But you can't be sure it has been stolen, can you?"

"Somebody doped him," Fairfield said pointedly. "We can be very sure of that. And they must have had a reason."

Pudsey's face became even greyer. "The doctor wouldn't, and neither would George Blake. Brian might, because sometimes he does the very last thing you'd expect him to, but this time he couldn't, because he's been locked up ever since tea, and Clara's been with him all the time, and that leaves only you and me, Mr. Fairfield, and me, I've got form."

Fairfield hadn't heard the expression before. "You've got what?"

"Form. You know." The other gestured impatiently. "A record. I've done time. Years ago, when I was little more than a kid. Three months for shoplifting."

"You could have a record as long as your arm," Fairfield reassured him, "but that wouldn't alter the fact that you couldn't have done this, because you've been with me for the last few hours."

"I know that," Pudsey said bleakly; "you know that, but nobody else does, and if this does end up with the fuzz, it's me they'll come down on, and if you start talking alibis that can't be checked, they'll be down on you as well. I know; I've had some."

"I don't share your distrust of the police," Fairfield said grimly, "but I can quite see how things could get complicated. I reckon it might be a good idea if we did something about bringing our friend here back to life to see if he can throw any light on things."

He patted Maskell's cheeks, lightly at first, as if afraid of hurting him, and then harder, much harder. And when that produced no effect, he took hold of the shoulders and raised them enough off the bed to be able to shake them vigorously. After a while, breathing heavily, he lowered the unconscious Maskell again and turned to Pudsey to ask: "You any ideas on the subject, Albert?"

Pudsey shuffled his feet and coughed. "If it's the same stuff that Brian has to take—" he started diffidently.

"It was the other times, so it's bound to be the same now. What's on your mind?"

"Only there's some other stuff I have to carry round with me in case Brian ever takes an overdose and goes off into a coma. Dr. Deakin gave it to me, and to Clara, and showed us how to use it, and if Brian faints, we have to give him some right away. He never has yet, though. Fainted." Pudsey produced a small white-metal box from his pocket, opened it and regarded the rubber-capped phial and syringe it contained with disfavour. "I never have trusted these things."

"Well, now's the time to get in some practice," Fairfield said cheerfully, and took hold of Maskell's limp left arm. "The usual place, I suppose." He started rolling up the pullover sleeve.

Taking out a pair of dark-rimmed spectacles, Pudsey adjusted them one-handed on his face and then held the syringe against the light while he studied the markings on its glass barrel before piercing the rubber cap with the needle and drawing up some of the phial's contents.

Fairfield grinned at the intensity of the display. "We'll make a doctor of you yet, Albert. Right, your patient's ready."

Pudsey, syringe poised over Maskell's bared upper arm, regarded Fairfield doubtfully over the tops of his glasses. "I only hope we're doing the right thing . . ."

"If it's supposed to help Brian, I don't see how it can harm our friend here. Go ahead, Albert, bung it in."

Pudsey managed to get the needle in on the third attempt. Fairfield's graphic shudder wasn't wholly feigned. "I felt that myself." He rolled the pullover sleeve down again. "How long is it supposed to be before we see some results?"

"I don't know." Pudsey put the syringe and phial back in the box, the box back in his pocket. "He didn't say. Dr. Deakin. I don't think he thought we'd ever have to use it."

"Nothing immediate, anyway." Fairfield raised Maskell's eyelids. "Still out cold. We'll just have to wait and see." He yawned widely. "Christ, it's been a long, hard day." He licked his lips. "A drop of something wouldn't be amiss." And brightened. "There's beer downstairs. Lager, anyway. Fancy a drink, Albert?"

Pudsey's acceptance was saloon-bar gentility itself. "I wouldn't say no, Mr. Fairfield. Shall I—?" He made a polite move towards the door.

"I'll go, old son. I know where it is. I'll take a look round at the same time; make sure everything's all right down there. You never can tell these days." Torch in hand, Fairfield whistled his way along the passage and down the stairs.

Pudsey sighed, looked round for a chair, saw there wasn't any and lowered his solid bulk onto the edge of the bed, carefully hitching up the knees of his blue serge trousers. He was sitting there, large hands resting on large knees, when Fairfield returned empty-handed.

"I can't bear it, Albert. He must have drunk it all. Sorry and all that." Hands in pockets, he leaned against the side of the dressing table. "All quiet down there. Well, it makes a change. Spotted his briefcase"—nodding at Maskell—"Didn't know whether to bring it up or not. It's the stuff he's been working on. Pretty important, I think, from what he said. Although, whoever it was shoved that last lot of dope in him mustn't have thought so—that's if it was papers they were after—it's just lying there for anyone to take. Or maybe we showed up before they had time to snaffle it. Anyway, I didn't see how it would have been much safer up here with us, so I left it where it was."

Pudsey hauled a fat brassy watch by a length of chain from one of his waistcoat pockets. He inspected it worriedly. "I'll have to be getting back, Mr. Fairfield. Nearly half past two; I never realised it was that time. I can't leave Clara on her own with him too long. He's not been used to being cooped up at night since we've been here; he's got used to wandering about."

Sucking in his breath, he replaced the watch, then came grunting to his feet. "I'm sorry, Mr. Fairfield, to be leaving you like this, but this is the first night since coming out here, three weeks back, that we've had to keep him up, and he won't be taking kindly to it. Not"—hurriedly—"that I'm afraid of him turning nasty. That's something he never 'as done, not in all the years he's been with us. But he gets fidgety, and has to be played with, like a kid. We have to ask him questions, make like we're on stage, you know?"

"This treatment he's having," Fairfield said sympathetically. "Is it having any effect, do you think? Can you see any change in him?"

Pudsey considered the question gravely. "It's 'ard to say, really, Mr. Fairfield. We don't actually see what he's like when the doctor's working with 'im. He takes Brian over to his place every morning for this special treatment, and keeps him there till evenin'."

He paused, thought, shook his head.

"In all fairness to Dr. Deakin, I can't see 'im getting better, not after all this time. You see, it's in his blood, as you might say, like some of us has black hair and some of us brown. It's the way we was made. We've often thought, me and Clara, that Brian must have took after one of his parents, whoever they might have been. Dr. Deakin has tackled something that's too much for him, I think. He's going to write about what he's doin', so he said. A thesis, he called it. At least, if it's not doing Brian any good, it's not doing 'im any harm. If I thought for one minute it was, even with what Deakin's paying us, I'd call it off like a shot."

He repeated that declaration very firmly. "Money or not, Mr. Fairfield, like a shot."

"You'd better get back—" Fairfield only just stopped himself in time from saying "home." No matter what little luxuries you gather about you, no matter how comfortable you make it, a hole in the ground with observation slits for windows can never be called that.

"Ay." The other looked down at Maskell. "I 'ope he'll be all right."

"His colour's better and his breathing's easier. Don't worry, Albert, he'll be fine. I'll hang about until he comes round, see what sort of mood he's in, if anything else has been happening to upset him, and then cope the best I can. I'd be mighty obliged if you could come round again as soon as it's light. I want him to see you as you really are, in the flesh."

"I'll try," Pudsey promised.

Fairfield handed him the torch. "You'll need this crossing that bloody moor out there."

When Pudsey had gone, stumping away down the passage and down the stairs, he stood for a few moments looking down at Maskell, trying to persuade himself that his colour was indeed improving, then turned, looking for somewhere to sit, as Pudsey had earlier done, and, like that stolid individual before him, finding nothing, lowered himself to the side of the bed.

The side of his head was aching, a monotonous steady throbbing that was so deliberate each oncoming wave of pain could be anticipated. He was dead tired, his eyes were sore and it was ages since that snack in the bunker affair where they were living. Living . . . Pigging, more like. He wondered just how much Pudsey and his wife were being paid for all this. And he wondered too what sort of man—a doctor, for God's sake—would pay out good money just for the opportunity of experimenting—no other word —with a loony type under conditions of isolation and control, whatever that was supposed to mean.

A strange sort of setup, all this. He knew from what Pudsey had told him that what was going on over in their little neck of the woods had nothing at all to do with Maskell being here; they'd been surprised to find someone was in the house. And as for Maskell—well, whoever had been responsible for having him dumped out here couldn't have had an inkling that somebody else had had the same idea of using this little cutoff bit of the world for a bit of tricky business. Otherwise, they'd have found someplace else. Ironic, when you came to think . . . Here was one bloke doing his best to make a loony type sane, and another bloke—if Maskell was to be believed—trying to turn a sane type loony.

And now the two different goings-on had sort of got themselves so tangled up that you couldn't make sense of any of it. Like who had coshed him—Fairfield gingerly touched the side of his head—and why. Like who had been pumping dope into the poor sod here on the bed.

And, turning to look down at that poor sod on the bed, to see if there was any change, Fairfield's glance fell on the hand that lay across the chest. His eyes narrowed a little. Picking up the hand he turned it in his fingers like a demonstration piece in a dissection laboratory, puzzling over the black rims of the nails and the way more blackness had become etched in the lines of the palms. And only the one hand, the right, was in that condition.

"Muck from the marsh?" he wondered aloud. But with only the one hand affected, that didn't seem likely. And it wasn't that sort of dirt. Somewhere at the back of his mind was another pair of hands that matched this one here now. Long-ago hands . . . his father's hands. Funny how you can forget, until something jogs your memory, how your own father's hands used to look. And his father had been a miner.

But this wasn't coal dust. Almost, but not quite. Something softer, not gritty. Soot. Maskell had had that hand of his somewhere that was covered with soot. And out here in the wilds, the only somewhere that could be was up a chimney. One of the oldest hiding places under the sun. And if Fairfield wasn't much mistaken, someone else before him had held that sooty hand just like he was doing now, and, having read its story, as he had done, had let it fall so that it had ended up in the same peculiar twisted position as it did when he let it fall now; the same position it had been in when he had first found Maskell lying here.

So the precious papers *had* found a new hiding place. Certainly not the fireplace down in the kitchen here, with fires being lighted in it all the time. Maskell had been making for the village when he had bolted out of the house that time. Somewhere in the village, then . . . Christ, talk about needles in haystacks. They had chased after him, to try and catch him up, but with the moon going in and out like a bloody theatre sign they'd given up and decided—at least Fairfield had decided and talked his companion into it—to try another way of getting Maskell sorted out.

A pound to a penny the papers had been stuffed up one of the fireplaces in the village, and the odds were that the man, or men, had worked it out just as he had done and were at this very moment going through each building in turn, sticking their mitts up every bloody chimney they could find.

Fairfield shifted uneasily on the edge of the bed, changing his position but finding the new one equally hard against the backs of his thighs. If he was going to stay here all the damn night he needed something better than this. Like one of the chairs from out of the kitchen. Even better, how about the bed next door, the one the chap named Howard had used. The way he was feeling, secondhand sheets didn't mean a thing.

Maskell, who had regained consciousness a few minutes earlier, watched from under his lashes as Fairfield went out of the room, taking the lamp with him.

THIRTEEN

His head felt heavy and slightly muzzy, and the upper part of his left arm was stiff and sore. Otherwise, Maskell felt fine. He wriggled up the bed until he was sitting with his back propped against the wall, mystified that it was still dark, when by the way he felt, as if he had had a long and refreshing night's sleep, one would have expected it to be the broad daylight of another morning.

But it was still dark outside. And inside, Fairfield having taken the lamp with him. And the house was silent now after the creaking of bedsprings in the next room. Fairfield, it seemed, had turned in for the night. Or what was left of it. The faint moonglow that floated in through the tall Georgian window wasn't enough for Maskell to make out the outline of his watch, let alone the time.

The last time he had checked the time had been while he was eating cold beans. That had been around half past one. He wondered how long he had been asleep. He wondered why Fairfield had come back to the house. He wondered if he was alone, or if his friend in the black cloak was somewhere about. And he wondered too if it was Fairfield and Black Cloak who had lifted him off the floor and laid him on the bed. He could quite distinctly remember dropping the cup of coffee before keeling over, the hard floor coming up to meet him. Tiredness, the cause of that flaking out? He didn't think so. But it hadn't been like the other times. No colour distortions or floating windows. Just going out, like a light being switched off.

He swung his legs to the floor, wincing as his left arm took his weight. It had been all right, that arm, before the blackout. And it was an odd sort of place to get bruised if it had happened when he fell. He winced again as he rolled up the sleeve. There was a bruise right enough, and with a minute red speck at its centre. And while he had never suffered bruises on that particular place before, he had seen red specks there, many times, having travelled often in his work to those countries where certain inoculations are obligatory. So, while he was asleep someone had given him an injection. Whatever it had been it didn't seem to have done any harm. If anything, his faculties seemed sharper than normal. At a guess he would say that, either asleep or unconscious—he didn't know which—he had been given a shot of something to make sure he stayed that way for some time longer. And the only reason he could think of why they should want him out of the way for a guaranteed interval was to give them time to search the house for the papers. Which, Maskell smiled to himself in the darkness, they would have failed to find. So Fairfield, one of the party, had been left on watch to give notice of when the victim came round and, the gloves now being off, was in a position to answer questions—under pressure if need be. Which was all very dramatic and cloak-and-dagger, but it did seem to fit present circumstances.

It was possible that Fairfield was the only one of them presently in the house. And he, it would seem, had fallen down on the job and succumbed to tiredness. Which was very handy. Seated on the edge of the bed, Maskell mentally listed available weapons. His iron rail should still be downstairs somewhere; in the kitchen, he fancied. And in the kitchen too were the heavy poker and the large table knives. But he would prefer not to go downstairs just in case there was another of them lurking about down there.

His gaze lighted on the dark bulk of his two suitcases. On one knee, he opened the larger of the two, groped under clothing of some kind for his leather toilet case, opened it by feel, and by feel slid out the pair of quite long-bladed scissors. A woman's weapon. He hoped that Fairfield, roused from sleep, would mistake the pointed steel for the blade of a knife.

He went silently out into the passage. The door of the adjoining room was half open. Fairfield's breathing was loud and regular. The lamp on the dressing table had been turned as low as it would go without going out. After the almost complete darkness of his own room, there was more than enough light now for Maskell to clearly see Fairfield, lying on top of the bed, fully dressed except for his shoes, those untidily upside down on the floor where he had kicked them off. Maskell turned the lamp up as far as it would go. Fairfield's head was sideways on the pillow, and the side uppermost was that from which the bruise and broken skin had so miraculously vanished. In close-up, it was easy to see how that miracle had been achieved. The patch of plaster covering the area was, in fact, beginning to peel away on one side, exposing the purple beneath. Some kind of thin plaster had been used—onionskin, was it called?—and then, to further disguise that covering, make-up had been applied thickly so that, from a distance, the illusion, as Maskell knew from experience, was complete. Someone had taken a deal of time and trouble to add just that one item to the list of incomprehensibles.

He laid the closed blades of the scissors—the handles hidden in his palm—across the sleeping man's throat, and brought his weight down heavily on the side of the bed. The small earthquake jerked Fairfield, blinking, back to life, seeing Maskell first, and starting to smile, then feeling the cold of the steel, at which touch his eyes came together over the bridge of his nose as he tried to squint down to find the cause. Maskell allowed him one brief glimpse. "Christ Almighty," Fairfield breathed, and stopped trying to push himself upright.

Maskell tried not to sound like a character from a third-rate movie when he said the only thing it seemed possible to say: "I think it's time we had a little chat."

At which Fairfield smiled faintly and relaxed, his eyes fixed on Maskell's. "I'm your man," he said. "You might not believe it, but I've been chasing after you since God knows when just to have a little chat." He blew heavily through his nose while his eyes did their best to meet again. "You can take that thing away, whatever it is. I won't move. Too bloody tired, for one thing." He tried to grin, but gave up when Maskell, instead of taking the steel away, pressed a little harder.

"So help me," Fairfield said earnestly. "I'll tell you everything I know. At least about my part in all this. I was going to, anyway. I even managed to persuade Pudsey to come and show himself to you, in case you didn't believe me; and if you hadn't bolted, we could have had your little chat then and there'd have been no need for this. Take it away, man, and let me sit up. I can't talk lying down. Damn it, I can't even breathe properly. Be reasonable. I swear I won't make a run for it or anything like that. I've no reason to."

Maskell kept the blades where they were. "Who is Pudsey?"

The other sighed. "Albert Pudsey. Here with his daughter Clara and a certain Brian Yarrow whom you've had the pleasure of meeting on—let me see—is it two occasions? You'll like Albert. Decent sort of bloke. I thought it was him that time when I got coshed. Someone outside called to me to go and join them, and I thought I knew who it was, so out I went, and whammo, curtains for yours truly."

"You went outside, just like that?" Maskell asked incredulously.

The other grinned weakly. "I'm not such a mug as it must seem. I thought the someone outside was here on the same job as me, and wanted to exchange notes, like."

"The same job?" Maskell wondered coldly.

"I want to tell you all about it. Honest. But from the start would be best—not in bits and pieces and having to go through parts of it twice."

He seemed earnest enough. Maskell took the scissors from his throat and slipped them into his pocket.

"That's better." Fairfield blew a hugely exaggerated sigh of relief. He wriggled up the bed until he could sit with his back against the wall. "That was a bad time you gave me. The stuff Albert pumped into you certainly did the trick. It's what he has to give Brian if ever he flakes out. We figured that if it doesn't hurt Brian, it couldn't hurt you." And when Maskell's hand went involuntarily to his bruised upper arm: "Ay, a bit of an amateur, our Albert. More at home with a dart board, I reckon. Still, it brought you round, and that's what we were after."

He reached up to touch the side of his head, found where the plaster was starting to peel away and smoothed it back into place. "Better keep this on for the time being, even though it isn't very comfortable. Albert's idea. He was sure it was Brian who bashed me; nobody else it could have been. And if I happened to meet Doc Deakin, he would spot the bruise, know who must have done it and might get windy and call the whole thing off. Which wouldn't suit Albert, who would lose a good steady income and have to go back on something he calls the Northern Clubs Circuit. Well, maybe it was Brian who did for me, but I've never heard him speak, so I can't say if it was his voice I heard outside."

Fairfield paused, shrugged, pulled a face and folded his arms in a resigned fashion across his chest.

"Well, I said I'd tell you all about it, and so help me, I will. It's nasty. It stinks. I very nearly told you what was going sometime back when I thought there were others out here on the same lark as me, and things were looking very nasty. Well, I know better now. Albert and his crowd are here for a very different reason—nothing at all to do with you. But the trouble is, the effect it's all had on you is just the same as if they'd been deliberately working on you. And I'm not going to be party to pushing a decent bloke over the brink, whether or not the bulk of the pushing has nothing to do with me."

Maskell said slowly: "You're trying to say that some of the things that have happened haven't been intended for my benefit at all, but some have, and those you're responsible for."

Fairfield smiled faintly. "In a nutshell. I plead guilty to a telephone ringing and some disembodied voices, poor things both, but mine own.

"It really all started about ten days ago. The boss, back home in the office, took me to one side and said he had a very delicate job for me, and if I pulled it off to the satisfaction of certain higher-ups, I'd be well in line for a tasty promotion. Ay-ay, I thought—checking the accounts in the Aden office. But that wasn't it, thank God. That would have been even worse than this. No, I was to be seconded first of all to our parent firm, Biddulph Electronics." He paused expectantly.

"Go on," Maskell said shortly.

"Off I went. I don't know the name of the man who talked to me there. Ordinary sort of bloke; the sort of face that is so everyday it slides out of your memory. He told me it was all very confidential, and that my whole future with the firm depended upon my discretion and the way I handled the assignment. That's what he called it—an 'assignment.'

"He said that the members of an unnamed board of directors were divided over the suggested promotion of a certain junior executive. To settle the matter they had all agreed to his being subjected to a kind of aptitude test, about which he would know nothing, to find out what he was made of and how he would react under conditions of stress. He was to be isolated, then set a problem, and it was to be up to me to create the conditions of stress. And I was to be on my own. There would be nobody but the two of us within a radius of some thirty miles."

"And you believed all that?" Maskell wondered.

"I believed him because I'd heard before that that sort of thing did go on up there in heaven where the Gods live. And what he dangled in front of my nose also helped. A three-grade promotion and a bonus you wouldn't believe. So I said yes. In my place, wouldn't you have done the same?"

"I suppose so," Maskell said.

"The telephone and the voices were his ideas. I made the tape of the phone ringing in my own office, and the voices tape in the Gents at Charing Cross Underground. Gave the right sort of hollow quality, I thought. The recorder's up there." Fairfield jerked his head at the ceiling. "You may have noticed that one of the baths has a lid over it. You just drop the lid, stand on it, reach up and push a board away, and there it is. I used an old alarm clock for a timing device. It's switched off now. I turned it off when I came back that time to find you flaked out at the bottom of the stairs. To tell the truth, I got the wind up, seeing you like that for the second time. I very nearly spilled the whole thing. I wish now I had."

Fairfield leaned hard back against the wall, his chin tight against his chest.

"You wouldn't credit how difficult it is to think up things likely to create confusion. Unless you have that sort of mind, I suppose; which I haven't. Stupid, the things I did. Like repacking your cases and bringing them back down to the hall. I suppose I must have had some idea of hoping you'd think you'd only imagined carrying them up and unpacking. Oh—and the clock. Brilliant. Changing the time. I didn't even know if you'd notice the bloody thing. But then the other things started to happen—the dishes being washed and stacked in that weird fashion. And then that couple you saw out in the moonlight. Real clever stuff that, I thought. Psychological. And I figured I wasn't the only one on the job after all, that the firm had sent out at least two others with the same brief. I figured wrong, of course. I'll come back to that later.

"They brought me here by chopper—oh, Christ, years ago. Five, six days back, anyway. I dossed down in the pub, hence the smell of cooking you spotted. In the daytime I hung about here in the house with a guy named Howard, waiting for you to show up. God knows why he wouldn't let me sleep here. Afraid of you showing up unexpected, I suppose, and catching me out. When we heard the chopper coming I set the recorder going, got the hell out of it, then came back to change the tape later when you were busy. It wasn't my idea to show up as an innocent bystander. Too nasty for me, that one. Came from the bloke who did the briefing. To really get things going, he said juicily, by making you think you were the only one to hear the sounds, and so get you doubting yourself. The acid test, he said. I made a disturbance out front in the hope of being spotted and invited in. If it hadn't worked, I'd have knocked at the front door and invited myself in, which wouldn't have looked so good."

Fairfield paused, brow furrowed pensively. "I think that's all. Yes, that's my little lot. Bang goes my promotion and bonus, and if I'm not much mistaken, bang also goes my present job. You wouldn't have an opening for a bright young man in your mob?"

"One prepared to do anything if paid enough?" Maskell wondered dryly, and then regretted the words the moment they were out.

"Don't be so bloody supercilious," Fairfield growled, stung.

"Everyone does everything for money. It's only a matter of degree. You and me, all of us out here. Albert and Clara. Even the doctor—he's told Albert he's going to write a thesis. Which he'll probably turn into money in due course. Brian's the odd one out, and he's a dummy. And look, high-and-mighty Maskell—"

He leaned forward, forefinger stabbing inches from Maskell's chest. "Don't forget you're only guessing this isn't an aptitude test like the man said. How can you be so bloody cocksure he was lying?"

Maskell leaned back from the stabbing finger. "Because I'm at the top of my heap," he said coldly. "Because I can't go any higher, either in my own department or in any other. Which makes a test pointless."

"Unless it's to make sure you're fit to stay at the top of the heap," Fairfield suggested slyly.

Maskell refused to rise to the bait, if bait it was. He changed the subject for one he had been waiting to discuss ever since hearing a certain name. "You mentioned someone named 'Clara'—"

"Did I?" Fairfield, being resentful, seemed in the mood for being awkward. "So I did."

"Would she sometimes be called 'Selena'?" Maskell wondered, and the other looked disappointed. "Where the hell did you get hold of that?"

"Sevin and Selena," Maskell said, making it sound like the music-hall turn it so obviously must be.

"Mind Over Matter," Fairfield, accepting the inevitable, finished the thing off. "But how the hell—?" His face cleared. "Brian?"

"We had quite a long chat."

"And got him soused into the bargain. His breath stank like a bleeding brewery. We had to lug him part of the way back to the bunker. You should have heard old Albert swear. They never have let him have beer, and right now they're under strict orders to keep anything of that nature away from him while he's on this LSD stuff Deakin's pumping into him. There's a rumour LSD and alcohol don't mix."

"I worked that out for myself. But by then it was too late. I'm sorry. I like Brian."

"You surprise me"—sarcastically. "But I'm damn sure Deakin won't like you if ever he finds out what you did. He can be a real tough customer, says our Albert."

"Five people," Maskell said. "Albert and his daughter. Brian. The doctor and someone called George."

"Calling the roll?" Fairfield grinned. "So Brian told you about George as well. I've not had the pleasure of meeting him yet. Or the doctor. But five it is."

"And you say their being out here has nothing at all to do with me?"

"You're not as important as you figured," the other said. "No, pure coincidence that the site someone chose for your little do was the same one Deakin chose for his—experiment, I suppose you could call it.

"Used to be an Army training ground, all this lot, so Albert informed me. No. 6 S.V.T.A. What does it stand for again. Specialised Vehicle Training Area. Hence the churned-up roads and the target bunker where Albert hangs out, and the better-class one the Army used to use for visiting V.I.P.s where Deakin and George Crowther are pigging it. The house itself used to be the Command Centre. One observation post was up in the church tower. According to Albert, the Army have been in and out of the place like a yo-yo. They first took it over during the last war as a temporary training area, gave up when the war ended, and most of the villagers came back again. God knows what they used to do for a living. Peat, maybe. Albert says there used to be sheep here, too. Then some years later the German Panzers came to South Wales to train, and the British units in those parts had to find somewhere else, so back they came up here again, saying this time it was to be for keeps. So the people moved out for good, taking everything moveable with them, even the church pews, even some of the stiffs out of the churchyard. And then, ten years or so later, the Army packs up and leaves again. Seems it was in all the papers at the time. That's how Deakin first came to hear about the place. Maybe that's how your bloke found out about it too. Anyway, it was about a couple of years back that the Army moved out for the last time—" Fairfield broke off. "You all right?"

The floor had quite suddenly gently rocked under Maskell's feet. The walls had momentarily surged in on him. He lowered himself to the side of the bed. The vertigo spasm passed. "I'm all right," he said.

"Good." But Fairfield, peering concernedly into his face, shook his head. "You're sure? Only you've had a rough do, one way and another. It's the LSD stuff of Brian's that gave you all that trouble. Not the pure stuff, apparently—a derivative. And Albert, you might be interested to know, says it must have been Brian who gave you the dope. Seems he actually confessed— Brian—to dishing out the second lot. He'd got hold of the idea that you were ill, and figured that what had done him good would help you. So he got some of his medicine, as he calls it, high-tailed it over here and laced whatever you were eating or drinking at the time. He says he didn't give you the first lot, and maybe he's telling the truth. And this last time, too, when Albert and I found you here on the bed. Albert says it must have been Brian. He says there's no one else for thirty miles but the two of us and the five of them, and the intelligent four of the five don't know you, have never had anything to do with you, and would much rather you'd never showed up in the first place. So why, says he, should any one of them want to harm either of us?"

"Because we're in the way," Maskell hazarded.

"That's what I thought. But a bit drastic, don't you think, this"—touching the side of his head—"and what someone tried to do with me when they lugged me away afterwards. You don't know about that, do you? Well, when we were up the church tower and you spotted the gent in the black cloak, well, I saw him too, but I made like I didn't because I figured he must be here on the same lark as me. So I slipped away to try and have a word with him, exchange notes, like, but I couldn't find him. But then later on, when someone out in the dark asked me to step out for a chat, well, I figured it must be him with the same idea. So I went out. And you know something? It was only by luck it wasn't a damn sight worse. It would have been if it hadn't been bright moonlight. I saw his shadow, the bastard, just in time, his hand up over his head. Couldn't see what he had in it. If I hadn't tried to sidestep it would have caught me right across the back of the neck. And that, let me tell you, might have been very nasty.

"Anyway, I passed out, like you know, and the next thing I know I'm being dragged across the bloody moor somewhere. I'm dropped on something soft, for which I'm grateful, ignorant sod that I am, and the next thing after that I know, I'm looking up at Albert and Clara all togged up for Brian's benefit in their stage clobber. They took me to their bunker and cleaned me up and put this plaster over the mark. And Albert said the place where I'd been dumped wasn't all that healthy, being something of a cross between bog and quicksand. And if they hadn't been out looking for Brian, well—"

Fairfield's shrug was expressiveness itself. "I can't believe Brian would have done something like that, even though Albert would have it that there was nobody for it but Brian."

Maskell said: "Just before you and Albert showed up here earlier, somebody attacked me. And at the time of the attack, Brian was either asleep or unconscious on the settee."

"Which makes at least one thing he can't be blamed for," Fairfield observed with satisfaction. And: "Someone had a go at you?"

"Tried to have a go. Only I got in first. He turned and bolted. It was too dark for me to see what he looked like. But he smelled like a doctor's surgery."

"Did he, by Christ," Fairfield breathed. "Like I said, there's more going on than Albert knows about. Oh, he's genuine, is our Albert. I'll stake my life on that. The only reason he's been blaming Brian for everything is not because he wants it to be Brian, but because he's so all-fired sure it can't be anyone else. Look, I'll give you the background to why Albert and the rest are here, just as Albert told me.

"As you know, he and Clara are on the stage. Sevin and Selena, Mind Over Matter. A sort of take-off of a proper mind-reading act. It starts serious with Clara, all togged up like you saw her that time, going down among the audience to hold up articles for Albert to identify. And he's blindfolded, and dressed to kill as Dracula, even wearing built-up shoes to boost his height. They use a code that is so obvious the audience latch on to it right away. Then Albert starts making mistakes and the whole thing becomes slapstick, with Albert seemingly desperately anxious to save the act, having a stab at everything from hypnosis to curing bunions.

"They've been touring the act ever since Albert's wife died six years ago, when Clara was only sixteen. Which makes her a fulsome twenty-two now, if you're interested. She's not a bad sort of lass. Anyway, they were a very poor third-rate act, mostly doing the smaller workingmen's clubs and the like. Well, it seems they were booked as one of the turns in a show given at an orphan asylum at a place called—Albert did tell me—St. Aspel. Being mostly kids in the audience, they really hammed it up—Albert's word, that—finishing up with their version of how a brain trust can go sour. Not very clever, as Albert says, but good for the odd belly laugh. Well, there's Clara down in the audience, making a mess of relaying the questions for the expert, Dracula, as ever was, to answer in any way he could. And there was one about what day did Christmas fall on in seventeen thirty-six or something, and Albert concentrates really hard and says Thursday, and this querulous voice from the back says timidly: 'No, it weren't, it were a Friday,' and everyone fell off their seats laughing.

"The upshot of which was next day Albert had words with the superintendent of the asylum, who seemed quite pleased to have one of his inmates, who was not only weak in the head but also overage, taken off his hands. And that's how Brian came to join Sevin and Selena. They used to sit him in the audience every night, and Clara used to give him the wink when to do his interrupting bit. It wasn't what he said, it was the way he said it that got the laughs. And like Albert pointed out to me, mostly audiences don't laugh at Brian, they laugh with him.

"They tried to teach him his part, but it was no go, he had to be left to go his own sweet way. They did try a rehearsal or two, but that was no go as well, not when they were out of costume, that is. They found out that when they were in ordinary clobber, Brian wouldn't have anything to do with the act. But the moment he saw them all dressed up, he was raring to go."

"Which is why they were wandering about here in the middle of the night in their stage outfits," Maskell suggested when Fairfield's pause seemed to invite such a suggestion.

"You're getting ahead of me now, but yes—that's what it was all about. Dressed like that, and Brian eats out of their hands. In ordinary clothes, and he's—what's the word?—recalcitrant." Fairfield grinned. "From Albert, that word; and he from Deakin.

"And he, the doc, came into it a couple of years back. They were giving their turn at a roadhouse, oddly enough not all that far from St. Aspel. After the show, this bloke comes round back to talk to them. Deakin, he says his name is, and he's a doctor specialising in mental conditions. He spends some time with Brian, goes away, comes back next day, has another session with wonderboy and then puts a proposition to Albert.

"He's very interested in Brian, says Deakin, and he would like a stab at testing him under conditions of isolation and control. No question of a permanent cure—he's honest about that, but given the right conditions, he thinks he might be able to help him. But the real point of the exercise is that he intends writing a thesis about it. And when Albert says no soap, Deakin starts talking money, real money—which is something Albert's never had in his life. So then he says yes, and Deakin says he'll let him know when he's ready to start, and agrees to pay Albert a retainer, and then about three weeks ago Deakin gets in touch with Albert again and says it's all systems go, and he's found just the place for the experiment."

"Experiment," Maskell echoed flatly.

"For want of a better word," Fairfield said. And once again the ground rocked under Maskell, and his eyes for a few moments lost their ability to remain under his control, sliding sickeningly away when he tried staring hard at the door.

He missed the first part of something Fairfield had been saying, catching: "—or anything to do with it at all. Just sheer luck—bad luck—that Deakin should have brought his weird little circus here just at the same time you were having your nerve tested, as it were. Bad luck for yours truly, too"—wryly—"like I said, down the drain goes bonus, promotion, and, I can't help feeling, also my job. All because I had a twinge of conscience."

Which didn't ring true to Maskell, wrestling with another spasm of vertigo. Priding himself upon being something of a judge of human nature, he didn't think that Fairfield was the type to sacrifice everything just for the sake of his conscience. Few men are, come to that. He was probably holding something in reserve, a trump card to be smugly produced to his employer on the day of reckoning—I only wised Maskell to the unimportant details—none of the important ones.

On the other hand—Maskell stared at a brown damp-stain on the wall that could at a stretch of the imagination be made into a hooknosed crone—he couldn't completely reject the possibility that this was indeed a kind of test to which he was being subjected—the purpose, as Fairfield had suggested—any significance there?—being to check his suitability for remaining in his present position. If that was the unnerving case, then he saw Pearson Agnew's hand behind it.

The vertigo finally passed. Maskell used his handkerchief to wipe his forehead, watched with growing concern by Fairfield. "Before you passed out this time, Maskell, did you have the same kind of hallucinations as the other times?"

Maskell, putting his handkerchief away, shook his head. "Nothing. Only a feeling of tiredness."

The other gnawed worriedly on his thick lower lip. "I was so damn cocksure it was the same. I hope to God I wasn't wrong, talking Albert into giving you that jab."

Maskell, too uneasy to harbour rancour, made an effort to speak lightly. "Time will tell, I suppose. And talking of time—how long is this test, if that's really what it is, supposed to last?"

"It's a test." Fairfield nodded wisely. "I have a feeling that bloke was speaking the truth. But he didn't say how long. Only that they'd lift me out by chopper—you too, I expect—when it's all over."

"And how will they know when it's all over?"

"Search me," Fairfield replied simply.

"No." Maskell shook his head. "No, I can't buy that. No, it must be something else."

"Something to do with those papers you stuffed up the chimney?" Fairfield asked innocently and unthinkingly, and then was startled by the fury with which Maskell swung on him, demanding harshly: "How the devil did you know about that?" And then, with passion quickly subsiding, giving way to perplexity: "How could you have known about that?"

For answer, Fairfield picked up Maskell's hand to point first at the black etch marks on the palm, then the black rims to the nails. "It didn't take a genius to figure out how they got like that." He paused. "And I'm not the only one. I have the feeling that right now at least one person, more likely two, are going through that village, chimney by chimney, and getting very sooty in the process."

The underground observation post originally designed to accommodate Important Visitors to the Vehicle Training Area was larger, better built and more comfortable than the smaller target observation bunker, presently occupied by Albert Pudsey and his party. It was equipped with an effective, if primitive, sanitary system, had running water, but lacked, as did indeed the entire area, electric power, having to make do with oil lamps and battery torches. It was divided into three main compartments which had temporarily been adapted to serve as sleeping quarters, the cooking and dining area, and what the man calling himself Dr. Deakin referred to in all seriousness as the "surgery."

A long, narrow room, the surgery, with slit windows through which colourfully uniformed high-ranking officers of emergent African nations had once gravely watched and selected the armoured vehicles for their emergent armies. But for the past three weeks it had housed a watching and waiting brief of a very different kind. A brief that had been an important part of the preparations for what had taken place there in the early hours of the new morning.

In his careful planning, Deakin had allotted a period of four hours to the special purpose that was to be the culmination of many months of preparation, and had wondered if he was being too optimistic. In fact, it had been satisfactorily accomplished in something under two hours, leaving only certain details to be cleared up before the mission could be declared as accomplished. Two things to be done, and done as swiftly as possible, for all the time there was in hand. Which was something George Blake knew, but: "I can get the briefcase back right away, Doctor—that'll only take ten minutes, but can't the papers wait till daylight? It's a hell of a walk to the village."

"We can forget we have time in hand," Deakin, on top of the world, replied with what was for him unusual patience. "There is a risk every second the papers are missing from where he hid them. The very essence of what we are doing is, as I have constantly tried to impress upon you, that it must be done without the slightest hint of anything untoward. As I have explained, to make full use of what has just been achieved will take at least three months. And during that time, nothing must happen to cause Saturn to change the code; otherwise all our work will have been wasted. We must assume, unlikely as is the possibility, that Maskell is at this moment toying with the idea of retrieving the papers from his chimney hiding place. So we must make certain they are there waiting for him. The briefcase is not nearly as important. If for some reason he does happen to need it, and can't find it, in his present state of mind he will assume he has moved it himself and has forgotten where. But as soon as you have replaced the papers, get the briefcase back into the house. And make sure nobody sees you."

"Fair enough." Blake, not present in the surgery during the crucial final stages, could hardly believe the thing had been successful. He asked again, for the third time: "It worked out all right? It's—all that's needed?"

Deakin opened the surgery door and left it open, endowing the action with an air of ceremonial finality. "I have everything I need," he declared.

Blake took down his coat from behind the door. It would probably be chilly outside. "I take my hat off to you, Doctor," he said fulsomely. Knowing what his share of the success was to be, he was in the mood to be lavish with compliments to the point of servility.

And Dr. Deakin, smiling his quiet smile of serene self-satisfaction, nodded and nodded again as he gazed down the vista of the future.

"We have a very great deal to thank my abacus for," he said.

⬛⬛ FOURTEEN ⬛⬛

Fairfield set his hands on Maskell's shoulders and pressed him gently back down onto the bed. There was little enough resistance to that pressure.

"You're not fit to go anywhere in your condition," he said. "It took you all your time then to get up on your feet. You'd never make it as far as the village."

"I've got to get those papers back before anyone else finds them," Maskell cried desperately, struggling ineffectually against the restraining hands.

"Take it easy." Fairfield took one hand away, the other being more than enough to hold the anguished Maskell down. "No need for panic. They can't have been gone all that length of time; there can't be more than two of them, surely, and God knows how many chimneys they'll have to search. Look—" He crouched down on his haunches. "It must be that stuff we pumped into you that's knocked the stuffing out of you like this. I'm sorry. You tell me which chimney, and I'll go get the papers for you. How's that?" Like a parent humouring a peevish child.

"No," Maskell said.

"All right." The other straightened back up. "Please yourself. The papers are out there somewhere, and we're here, and that's it. And what's so bloody important about them, anyway?"

As well as the weakness that had suddenly come to Maskell's body, a woolliness had come to fill his head, muffling his thoughts, making it difficult to concentrate. He couldn't remember if he had ever explained the significance of the papers to Fairfield. He thought he had; it seemed he couldn't have.

He relaxed, leaning sideways against the end of the bed. The lamp flickered to a sudden draught, shadows bunching in the far corners of the room.

"There's a code that Saturn's top senior directors use to transcribe certain information that must be available to their eyes only," Maskell started. Fairfield, one hand in his trouser pocket, the other on the side of the dressing table, listened without taking his eyes from Maskell's face.

It wasn't easy, Maskell found, to condense the significance of the code into a few words. He tried; he thought what he was saying made sense. He spoke of the vast amount of money that was involved, and his listener whistled softly.

"By an oversight on someone's part, a set of partially decoded figures came into my hands—"

"The papers?" Fairfield wondered.

"One sheet." Maskell nodded. "Plus two sheets filled with my efforts to break the code. A useful aid to anyone who finds them. The figures are useless as they stand, but if taken in conjunction with the mass of coded material in my briefcase, they could be used to break the code."

The other seemed to have grasped the situation surprisingly quickly. "And that's what you've been doing—trying to break the code. Like trying to work out a super anagram, yes?"

Which was quite an accurate assessment. Maskell raised his brows. "Something like. Yes, I did try to break it, but not because I wanted to line my own pockets. For a very different reason. But I couldn't do it. There's only one way it can be done using pencil and paper, and that way could take months."

"But if you couldn't manage it, why the concern for those papers? If they're no use to you, they're no use to anyone else."

"There are such things as mechanical aids," Maskell said dryly, and it was the other's turn to lift his brows.

"A computer?" he wondered.

Maskell nodded. "Months reduced to minutes. But the breaking down would have to be done without anyone knowing it had been done."

Fairfield understood why without having to be told. "If the enemy lays their hands on your code, you change it, pronto. But for God's sake, you're not suggesting someone's smuggled a computer out here?"

"I don't see how," Maskell said, "but I have to consider it. I'm assuming the only way of getting here is by air—"

"By chopper," the other confirmed. "And light chopper at that. Two-seater. Ground not suitable for anything heavier. I've had dealings with digital computers. Even if you could dismantle one of the smaller jobs and pack it into a globe-front chopper—which even Houdini couldn't have done—you still wouldn't have any electricity out here to operate the bloody thing once you've reassembled it. You can count computers out." Fairfield was very certain of that.

Maskell, not so certain. "It seems impossible on the face of it—"

"You're thinking maybe of one of those dinky jobs?" Fairfield flicked his fingers over the imaginary buttons of an imaginary pocket calculator. "You know?"

Maskell shook his head. "It would have to be something capable of handling combinations of letters and figures. They don't. No, I've been thinking in terms of reproduction. Photostats. Photographs."

Fairfield held an imaginary miniature camera to one eye, clicked an imaginary shutter and, instead of passing facetious comment about spies and false moustaches, suddenly became silent and worried, as if there had been something about the idea of miniature cameras that didn't appeal to him in particular.

"Someone could take pictures of your papers," he said slowly after a while, "take the film out with them, have it processed and blown up and then feed the stuff into a computer in their own good time. They could do that, couldn't they?"

"They could," Maskell agreed, "but I don't think that's how it would be done. It would be far too risky. Assuming they are able to lay their hands on my papers long enough for them to be photographed without my knowledge, they can't be certain, until they start feeding the data into a computer, that they have sufficient data to break the code. And before they start the feeding, they must first have arranged to have a particular kind of computer placed at their disposal, along with its operating team. There aren't very many of those, and the few there are are controlled either directly or indirectly by Saturn. Too many people would become involved. It would be impossible to keep the thing secret. I don't see how they could do it that way."

"You come up with ways in which it could be done," Fairfield said crossly, "then knock each down in turn. So I can't for the life of me see what you're so concerned about. For the record, you can take it from me there's no equipment of any sort out here. I've been inside both bunkers. Albert showed me round Deakin's while the doc was out. Not even a bleeding mousetrap. I can't see what the hell you're so worried about."

The lamp flickered to another draught. "A feeling—" Maskell told the dancing shadows. "A hunch, if you like. No, it's more than that. All this—" His spread hands encompassed everything that had been happening. "Either me or the papers. It's got to be one or the other."

"But you told me it was only by an accident that those partly decoded figures came into your hands," Fairfield said. "I take that to mean that nobody else knew about them but you. Until now, that is, and then only me. So what the hell?"

"That's my hunch," Maskell said bleakly. "I don't think that paper was an oversight after all. I think it was deliberately planted on me."

"Deliberately planted?" The other stared at him. "I don't get it." He shook his head. Then his expression changed. "Using you as a stooge, is that what you're getting at? It was supposed to look like it came into your hands by accident, and you weren't on the ball and let it slip through your fingers into the wrong hands. Is that what you mean?" His dismay, certainly unfeigned, seemed out of all proportion in someone who was himself in no way personally affected.

"If you're still willing to get them for me," Maskell said, "the papers are in the pub chimney."

Absorbed, it seemed, with some problem of his own, Fairfield didn't hear him the first time. Maskell told him again.

Then: "The boozer. I'll get them." Fairfield stopped at the door, turning to look back over his shoulder, shaking his head. "It seems that in our line of business, the closer you get to the top the filthier it gets. What a bleeding life. But you could be wrong thinking someone's gunning for you. You're only guessing." He seemed to take heart from that thought. "Me, I'd say it's much more likely it's what it's supposed to be—"

"An initiative test," Maskell said caustically.

"It doesn't sound so feasible when you use that tone. Still, what the hell." Fairfield grinned sideways. "I won't be long."

Maskell listened to his perhaps purposely loud progress along the passage, down the stairs and out through the slammed front door, then rested his head against the wall and closed his eyes. But when he felt himself drifting, sleep threatening, he opened them again with an effort, forcing himself as wide awake as the muzziness in his head would allow, not sure why he felt he must stay awake, obeying an instinct.

Five past four by his watch, held in the orange lamplight. Dawn couldn't be all that far away. About six, this time of year? He caught himself drifting off again, and this time pushed himself off the bed, collected the lamp and took it and its attendant shadows towards the top of the staircase.

The dark, indistinctly seen shape in one corner of the hall he took at first to be one of his briefcases, then realised it was far too large, and discovered it to be Fairfield's waterproof-covered pack, lying on its side. He couldn't remember where he had left the briefcases. One of them, the unimportant one, would be up in the bedroom. The other must be in the lounge.

It wasn't in the lounge. Shadows circled in the wake of the searching lamplight. Hadn't slipped behind either the settee or the chairs; or found its way into one of the corners. It must still be behind the fuse panel. Hand cupped over the top of the glass funnel to shield the flame from the night breeze, Maskell went out through the french window onto the terrace. No moon now; dark frozen turbulence overhead; a faint glow low on the eastern horizon. In the generator house of the onetime army occupation, the fuse panel hung loosely, the cavity behind empty.

He retraced his steps, stumbling over the verge of the terrace, staggering a little with a sudden small spasm of vertigo that had come with a sense of pressure inside his head.

The briefcase was in the lounge, where it must have been all the time—propped against one of the easy chairs—the one he had been using, drawn up still to the low coffee table. Putting the lamp on the table, Maskell lowered himself into its cold leather depths. He wasn't much concerned that he should have overlooked the case earlier; it seemed natural in his present condition that he should have. He dragged it up onto his lap to open it. The contents seemed intact. He leafed through the folders in a lackadaisical fashion, piling them by his elbow on the table. Force of habit, nothing more, made him pause reflectively at one sheet of figures, take out a pen and check a total. He moved on automatically to the next column, barely aware of his mind's functioning. He was still working when Fairfield returned, so involved he didn't look up.

"I saw your light from the road. Couldn't sleep?" Fairfield had the papers in his hip pocket. "Or were you too worried about these?" He tossed them on the table. "I told you they'd be safe enough."

The sheet he was working on disturbed, Maskell picked them up and leaned back in his chair to unfold and examine them.

Fairfield, hands in trouser pockets, approved the cluttered tabletop. "That's what I like to see. Keen. You been having another stab at code-breaking?"

Maskell wasn't sure why he felt he must study the papers so carefully. There was no way of telling from them if they had been abstracted from the chimney, unfolded, refolded, returned. At least there were no marks at the corners that might suggest they had been pinned down flat for photographing. He looked up. "Thanks. I'm grateful."

"You're welcome," the other replied laconically. "I asked if you were having another go at breaking the code."

Maskell leaned forward again to put the papers on the table. "I thought I'd explained that was impossible."

Fairfield took one hand from his pocket in order to rub the side of his nose. "You could be mistaken. I mean, about it being impossible. Couldn't you? Maybe there's something you've missed. Some sort of opening. Like the *Times* crossword. You get so far, then stuck. Dead end. No hope of doing any more. Then a sudden flash, and everything falls into place. I should have another shot at it if I were you." He sounded very much in earnest.

So much so that Maskell looked up from his casual studying of the now soot-dusty papers to stare very hard at the long face above the athletic-looking, thick rolled pullover collar. There could be no doubt that Fairfield, for some reason or other, did very much want him to have another attempt at code-breaking. To keep him occupied? he wondered.

"This isn't the *Times* crossword," he pointed out.

"It's the same sort of thing. Substitutions. Anagrams. You said so yourself. Moving pieces round till they fit." Fairfield was now making no secret of his anxiety that another attempt should be made. "Maybe, if you take another look, you'll find something you missed before. You know?"

What Maskell did know, because it was now so very obvious, was that the other knew something of significance about the code that he had not seen fit to admit. It would be waste of time, he felt sure, to ask outright what that something was. He had the feeling that Fairfield was on his side, was in his own way trying to help.

"Perhaps I will have another try," he agreed.

"That's the stuff," Fairfield approved with cheerful and slightly sickening heartiness, and yawned very loudly in show-off fashion. "And I'll go get myself a spot of shut-eye before the dawn comes up like thunder out of Ballachulish 'cross the moor." He reached for the lamp; stayed his hand. "Hell, no; you'll need that. Where's t'other one?"—and went off to look for it.

Frowning thoughtfully, Maskell watched his broad grey back melt into the darkness of the hall. Fairfield, with his own peculiar code of honour, had been trying to tell him something, to help him, and at the same time keep faith with whoever was employing him. That was the only construction Maskell could find to put on that little interchange. It was as if the other had said: "It can be done if you keep hammering away at it. There's a trick to it. I can't tell you any more, because I'm paid not to."

Maskell bent over the papers on the table. If that assumption was right, then there had to be something he had missed before, some minor detail that was the key to the whole thing. And carrying the assumption a stage further, the odds were that in that case this wasn't the Bluesheet code after all, but a simplified gimmicky version, perhaps specially thrown together for this occasion. Certainly—the idea hardening—put together for this test by the bright boys of Pearson Agnew's estate. And they had damn near got away with it. But for Fairfield, they would have.

Now that Maskell's mind had started working again, the muzziness was clearing. There was the beginning of a return of the strange machinelike clarity he had earlier experienced and put down to the aftermath of drugs. As it must be now: a delayed reaction to whatever it was Albert Pudsey had pumped into him—his hand strayed absently to his still sore left arm—or to whatever had been used before that to put him to sleep. According to Fairfield, Brian's watered-down brand of LSD. And apart from distorting the senses and causing hallucinations, wasn't that stuff paradoxically supposed to temporarily heighten perception and sharpen the mind? Which was why his own mind now was giving the impression of being a machine, waiting, purring over, to be switched on. And the very act of picking up a pencil and drawing a blank sheet of paper towards him was the switch that set the wheels moving.

Use the same hit-and-miss routine before, but this time watch out for combinations of figures and letters that seemed apart from the regular pattern. Unit column figures first. Each figure would be represented by a group of six letters and figures. Let X stand for the first digit in the unit column . . .

His mind had become, to all intents and purposes, an entity to itself, working independently, leaving him to be nothing more than a mere observer, sitting, it seemed, apart from himself, able to look over his own shoulder at what the pencil was writing. The room with its warm orange lampglow and bulky furniture shapes and dark corners grew faint about him, seeming to recede to another plane, leaving him sitting alone in some high faraway place.

So dreamlike had it become that when he did in fact fall asleep—his pencil coming to rest with its point still on the paper; his head drooping slowly to lie on his curved arm—the transition from reality to dream was unbroken, the work continuing without pause; only now, in his dream, the pencil had become unnecessary, the figures and letters and symbols flowing from the tips of his fingers as he moved them across the paper, filling the pages with glowing columns that marched and countermarched and took up station, on parade—one hundred combinations of six figures and letters—the one hundred groups that were the Saturn Bluesheets code.

And while Maskell slept and dreamed, and dreaming, solved his problem, in his bedroom, Fairfield put his oil lamp on the dressing table and lifted his pack, which he had collected on his way through the hall, onto the bed. The waterproof cover was an ex-army surplus groundsheet, fastened on with two leather straps. Inside was a green canvas haversack, also services surplus, secured with two buckled canvas straps. The haversack was fairly new, the straps stiff, and he bent his forefinger nail painfully back on one as he struggled to push it through the tarnished buckle. He swore under his breath, sucking the injured member while with the other hand he reached inside the haversack to draw out a radio transmitter from its nest of shirts, vests and rolled-up socks. Not a particularly modern-looking piece of equipment, the transmitter, but adequately functional, as he had already discovered, having tested it, as instructed, immediately upon his arrival at Kirkmalcolm. Now, with his assignment apparently nearing a reporting stage, he felt it would be just as well to perform a further check, to be on the safe side. It also appealed to his sense of humour that the man at the other end of the preset wavelength, whoever he was, would almost certainly be in bed and fast asleep and would not relish being roused at five in the morning to give the approved Roger Okay.

Humming to himself, Fairfield sat on the side of the bed, balanced the transmitter across his knees, extended the quite long antenna and switched on. He was somewhat disappointed when the voice at the other end gave no indication of being put out at being called at such an hour. Switching off, he returned the set to the haversack, pushed the whole lot under the bed, stretched to turn the lamp low, then lay back on the bed, closing his eyes, to fall asleep almost immediately.

When Maskell finally stirred awake, opening his eyes, he could feel the pencil still between his fingers, but his head was now resting, quite comfortably, against the cool leather back of the chair. It was broad daylight. It seemed to him in the first few confused moments of waking that it was an eternity since he had last seen sunlight. But sunlight it was now, in a patchwork of yellow rectangles on the dusty floor. And the oil lamp still burning; the flame itself invisible now, lost in the goldness, but with a faint smell of warm paraffin to tell it was still alive.

He yawned and stretched, the pencil falling from his fingers to go rolling away across the strewn papers. And across the paper he had been working on last night. The last time he had seen it it had been almost blank; empty but for his first few tentative calculations across the top. Now it was filled with figures and letters, neatly arranged in columns of groups of six. Not one hundred of them, as there had been in the dream, but eighty— which was the number there should be: the eighty complex symbols that constituted not some tricked-up substitute, but the authentic Saturn Bluesheets code.

His mind, dazed by sleep, started the return to normality. To the normality of reality and logic, not the drug-induced mechanical clarity of last night. Reason took over from automaton acceptance. He bent over the spider-thin writing that filled the sheet. And gradually, after a little while, he began to piece together a picture. He remembered things he had seen, things he had heard, things he had been told. And he also remembered— because having an interest in the queer side of life it had stuck in his memory—a newspaper article he had read years before about twins, born in America and blessed—if that was the word —with an unusual talent.

He put all these things together, and where they didn't match, where there were gaps, he tried to use logic and reason and guesswork to fill those gaps. He felt pretty certain he knew what it was all about. He knew that he had been used for another man's purpose. A stooge . . . Oddly, he felt no animosity towards the man who had so made use of him—if anything, something approaching admiration. He leaned back in his chair, his hands resting quietly on the worn broad leather arms. He was sitting so quite some time later—for washing and shaving and finding a change of clothes could wait—when Fairfield came into the room's sunlight, bouncily filled with the joys of the new morning. Stripped to the waist, the slug-whiteness of his flesh looked almost unhealthy against the dark fur on his chest and the purple bruise. He said something about the brightness of the morning, remarked, rubbing his chin, on the softness of the water.

And Maskell said, not making a question of it because now he knew it must be so: "You have some way of communicating with your employer."

The other lost his breeziness, stopped smiling and was patently embarrassed. "Ah. Yes. Well, now—"

"I'm assuming that your instructions are to contact him as soon as you're satisfied I've broken the code."

Fairfield, wary, gently rubbed his bruise. "You're only guessing that because of what—"

Maskell interrupted by lifting his hand from the sheet of spider writing. "You can see for yourself."

Fairfield made no secret of his delight. "I told you you could do it if you stuck at it." He came to bend over the paper, studying it as if the wavering columns made sense to him. Struck by suspicion, he looked up to ask anxiously: "You have done it? You're not trying to pull a fast one?"

"It's broken," Maskell assured him with suitable gravity.

"That's it, then. Now we can all go home. And I'm not bloody sorry. Yes, I do have a way of getting in touch with what you call my employer, sod him. A radio. You want to come and see me use it?"

"I'd prefer to use it myself."

"You mean, you be the one to send the assignment completed signal?"

"I mean, use it to contact somebody at my head office."

"Be my guest. But I hope you bleeding well know how to operate one of those contraptions because I bloody don't." And at Maskell's disbelief: "It's preset, the wavelength I have to use. All I have to do is switch on and speak. I wouldn't know how to change it if you were to pay me. You want to come and see for yourself?"

Maskell followed him upstairs to his bedroom, watched while the transmitter was dragged out of the haversack and placed on the dressing table with its antenna extended.

"All set." Fairfield unclipped a small hand microphone and pressed a switch. "Watchman calling. Watchman calling. Over." He flicked another switch, caught Maskell's eye and winked conspiratorially.

"Listener here," a voice said tinnily from the small speaker. "Over."

"Assignment Abacus accomplished," Fairfield said with due solemnity, repeated the message and then marred the occasion by catching Maskell's eye and winking again.

"No!" Maskell exclaimed sharply as the other reached to switch off. He snatched the microphone from him. "Hello? Who is this?" But whoever it was had switched off. The speaker buzzed emptily. "Damn." He slammed the microphone back in its cradle and then stopped to examine the front of the transmitter. If the large central knob was the tuner, then the tuning scale appeared to have been deliberately removed. "Damn," he said again.

"I don't know about you," Fairfield said, "but I don't know the first thing about these gadgets. I'm a clerk, not a bloody sparks. Was it urgent?"

"It'll have to wait."

"Not all that long, I shouldn't think. The bloke said the moment I sent in the mission accomplished signal he'd have the chopper in the air as soon as possible." He snorted. " 'Mission accomplished.' Christ. Someone had fun thinking that one up. I wonder where they got the name 'Abacus' from?"

"It's the coloured beads-on-wires gadget they use in kindergarten to teach very young children how to add and subtract," Maskell replied absently, engaged with other things. "They use larger ones for calculating in the Middle and Far East in shops and offices. I suppose an abacus is the earliest and simplest form of computer."

"I know what the bloody thing is," Fairfield said testily. "I just wondered why they picked on that name for this job?"

"Can you think of a better one?"

"Plenty." Fairfield telescoped the antenna and returned the transmitter to the haversack. "I suppose they'll lift you out first and then come back for me." He grinned. "Two different destinations. It just struck me—if you hadn't pulled it off, how long d'you reckon they'd have kept you out here before calling it a day and calling the test off?"

Without bothering to answer, Maskell went over to the window to look out. The sky was a clear pale blue, almost free of cloud. A broken line of long-necked birds flapped lazily away. He supposed the helicopter would come from the direction, from Oban, over the village. Agnew would come with it; he felt sure of that. To check to make sure the code had been broken, if nothing else. There were aspects of the affair that weren't as yet wholly clear, but Pearson Agnew's involvement, albeit unintentional—Maskell smiled to himself—just had to be a certainty.

Fairfield had come to join him at the window and, arms wrapped about his naked torso, was studying his face. "So not dirty work at the crossroads after all," he said tentatively. "Not like you were afraid of. It was a test after all."

"What's that?" Maskell came back to earth. "Oh—it was both. Test and dirty work, as you call it, both."

"Both? I don't get it. How the bloody hell could it be both?"

"One the excuse for the other." Maskell looked at his watch. Ten past ten. He decided not to hurry over washing and shaving and changing into more suitable clothes for his return to London. If Agnew arrived before he was ready, then he could damn well wait, and be in no position to complain. He had the feeling that there was after all no great urgency about getting a message through to head office. If he knew Agnew—who was efficient above all else—the moment Fairfield's mission accomplished message had been relayed to him, he would first be stunned, then disbelieving, but then, being so efficient, would immediately clamp down on any further usage of the current Bluesheets code, at the same time authorising the immediate formation of a replacement. Maskell smiled to himself again. One thing was also for sure: Pearson Agnew was going to have his vanity very badly bruised when he discovered how he had been taken for such a ride, and by someone who had no financial standing at all in the Saturn hierarchy.

The helicopter came slanting and gleaming out of the south some two hours later, touching down on the strip of coarse grass beyond the terrace, its solitary passenger climbing down, with the wind tugging at his clothes, while the rotor was still turning, to come at a stooping half-run towards the house, one hand clamped to the inevitable grey fedora.

Maskell, washed and changed and waiting, didn't go outside to greet Agnew. They met in the room with the leather chairs and settee, with the paper containing the broken code there on the low table for anyone to examine, so sure now was Maskell that its usefulness was finished.

Pearson Agnew, severe in city steel-grey, black hair as sleek as polished leather, white features as expressionless as always—they would show no emotion if the sun were to one morning rise in the west—took the sheet of spider writing in his solid white hands and studied it with great care.

"Yes." His faint sigh could have been the aftermath of his dash to the house. "I would have said this was impossible." And, looking up: "But not your writing, Boyd."

"It's a long story," Maskell said. "I assume you have taken the necessary steps?"

"I don't need to be reminded—" the other started coldly, and then broke off, tone and manner changing. "I cancelled all further use of the code before leaving my office." He held up the paper. "Whose writing is this?"

"At this stage I'd rather talk about the somebody else who has a copy of it," Maskell said. "The somebody who believed the copy he had managed to obtain was the only one in existence outside Saturn, that nobody apart from him and his confederate, a man named George Blake, knew about it; who believed that in his hands he held the key to a fortune. But who, I suspect, was very sadly disillusioned when he saw your helicopter touch down, knowing what that must mean."

Agnew, clearly knowing who was under discussion, allowed a touch of harshness to tinge his normal colourless voice. "For all the facts point to Sir John Mellish-Rae, I find it very hard to believe. Do you have proof? Have you seen him for yourself?"

"He took good care that I shouldn't see him. And no, I have no proof. But there is no one else it could be but Sir John. For the record, he's calling himself 'Dr. Deakin.'" Maskell smiled faintly. "A comedown, reducing himself from consultant to plain G.P."

"I can see how he was able to arrange things in this fashion," Pearson Agnew said greyly. "What I don't see is how he was able to break the code from the inadequate material that was available and without the services of a computer."

"The impossible task that was set me," Maskell said dryly.

"For the good of Saturn," replied the other evenly, with no apology, no regrets. "How did he do it?"

Maskell told him.

"A late lunch, arranged at the Stag in Oban," Pearson Agnew said a little later, wafer-thin gold watch cupped in white palm. "If you will give me the pleasure of your company." In the tone of one who didn't expect and was not prepared to take no for an answer. But a no he got, with an apology.

"I would like to." Maskell was sincere about that, understanding how Agnew had done what he had done not for any personal reasons but, as he had said, for the good of Saturn. "There are a couple of things I would like to clear up here first. Fairfield deserves an explanation, if only for the way in which he tried to help me. And there is somebody I would rather like to meet. Perhaps you could send the 'copter back to pick us up?"

Agnew adjusted his elegant fedora. "I will do that. And Sir

John—" He adjusted the hat, using his reflection in the french window. "No doubt he will have made his own arrangements for returning to town."

He then did Maskell the unusual courtesy, having adjusted his hat, of taking it off again in salute. "I look forward to seeing you in the board room tomorrow morning, Boyd."

FIFTEEN

"Albert said he had the feeling Deakin wasn't his real name," Fairfield said. "He's in for a shock when he finds out who he really is. Sir John—What was it again?"

"Mellish-Rae," Maskell supplied.

Fairfield mouthed the name. "Quite a ring to it. I've got the feeling I've come across it before. In the papers?"

"Or the magazines, the glossy variety." Maskell offered captions at random. "Socialite Surgeon at Ascot. Villa at Cannes. Round-World Dash to Bedside of Arab Multimillionaire. Whatever he does is news."

"And there he is, pigging out yonder in that bunker." The other shook his head in wonderment. "It takes some believing."

"For a very little discomfort," Maskell pointed out, "for a very short time, he stood to make himself a fortune to dwarf all fortunes."

They were in the pale sunshine of the terrace, Fairfield, hands stuffed in trouser pockets, sitting with long legs inelegantly splayed on the low wall. Maskell, wearing the dark-blue suit and striped shirt and white city collar of his arrival, leaned against a crumbling plinth that had probably once supported an urn.

"All this—" Fairfield gestured with his chin. "You say you had it all figured out even before Agnew showed up?"

"I'd like to be able to say I had some idea of it from the start," Maskell said. "But I can't. I knew something was going on—that was obvious—but none of my hunches came anywhere near the truth. At least I didn't take the story of a leak seriously. I felt certain it was just an excuse to call the special board meeting, and that there had to be another reason for the flap. It didn't occur to me until it was too late that the meeting itself was the excuse to get me out here. And to be honest, it wasn't until I woke up this morning and found that sheet of calculations in front of me that I started to put the pieces together. I remembered reading—ages ago—about the twins in New York, in their teens, and the odd things they could do.

" 'Idiot savants,' they call them. A term used for centuries—it's nothing new—to describe mentally retarded persons who possess a most unusual talent. For some reason that no one knows, they are able to perform very complicated and sophisticated calculations in their heads, quickly and accurately. And yet apparently they can come unstuck if asked to add two and two together.

"If they are asked on what day of the week a certain date, centuries ago, fell on, they are able to come up with the answer right away. It was remembering that in particular, and what you told me about Brian—how Pudsey first came to use him in the act—that gave me the first glimmering. The article said that experiments were being performed on certain idiot savants to see what effect certain perception-heightening drugs such as LSD derivatives might have on them. And I remembered you telling me that that was the sort of stuff Deakin had been feeding Brian. After that, everything more or less fell into place."

"Idiot savant." Fairfield frowned pensively. "It sounds vaguely familiar. Maybe I read the same article. And of course Sir John Whatsit would know all about that sort of thing."

"I don't think anything will happen to him," Maskell said, looking down at a polished toecap. "I think he will just be allowed to walk—fly, rather—out of here, and that will be an end of it. Except that Saturn in general and Conrad Earlam in particular will quietly dispense with his services. But to avoid publicity, he will never be charged, and so I don't suppose we will ever get to hear his version. But I don't think there can be much doubt about what happened.

"Purely by chance he saw Sevin and Selena doing their act with Brian. He probably realised straight away that Brian was an idiot savant, even though it seems they used to use him as comic relief, not because of his talents. I would think Sir John got his idea right away, and then clinched it after he had had the second session with Brian. All he had to do then was wait for the right moment.

"Which came when Conrad Earlam had his next attack. Sir John said gravely the time had come for Earlam to step down. If he didn't, the next attack could prove fatal. And who was to step into his shoes? Agnew told me this morning that the senior directors met to discuss the matter, with Sir John present as adviser. According to Agnew, wise after the event, the suggestion that a younger man should take over was put forward by somebody previously primed by Sir John. My name was proposed as the most suitable candidate.

"Then came the arguments." Maskell smiled a little. "I didn't need Agnew to tell me that. Brownlea for, Henderson and Agnew against, the rest equally divided, and Sir John, hovering in the wings and coming forward at the right moment to suggest a test. Which suggestion the board seized upon with relief as being the best way out of the impasse.

"And what form should such a test take? Another job for the expert on things psychological. Sir John had it all worked out, of course, and from what Agnew told me of them, they were passed on to you, almost verbatim, as your instructions."

"He told me that the code you were to try to break wasn't the pukka job, which you'd never get on top of in a month of Sundays, but a put-up affair, designed specially for the occasion." Fairfield moved his shoulders. "That's why I kept on at you to stick with it. And all the time it was the bloody real one you'd been lumbered with."

"Once the test was settled," Maskell continued, "Sir John took Agnew on one side and said that in his opinion I lacked the necessary experience. Agnew agreed—"

"You said before that that sod has his knife in you," Fairfield interrupted.

"I may have been doing him an injustice," Maskell said, looking up from his study of his shoe. "I think I'm inclined to believe him when he says there's nothing personal about it. Anyway, he went along with Sir John's idea of replacing the fake code with the real one, to make sure I failed the test, knowing that even with the page of calculations that was to fall into my hands 'by accident' I wouldn't be able to break the code. The test, incidentally, was in two parts; I was first supposed to figure out a reason why I had been dumped on my own in the wilds, then break down the code so that I could find the proof of my suspicions.

"And of course there had to be that important sheet of half-done calculations. Without its help, even Brian, working from scratch, wouldn't have got anywhere. Even a computer would have been useless."

Maskell paused. "And that was it. Sir John first flew in the Pudseys and Brian, and then came himself, along with George Blake—God knows where he got him from—the night after my arrival. It was the sound of his helicopter that woke me up and made me go to the window. All he had to do then was get hold of the sheet of calculations and the bulk returns in my briefcase long enough for Brian's drug-sharpened mind to work the oracle. But he had to do it in such a way that nobody, me in particular, had the slightest suspicion what was happening.

"He tried doping me with some of Brian's LSD to keep me out of the way for a while. I'm pretty sure that's what happened. Only Sevin and Selena, out looking for Brian, and knowing that in the fortnight they'd already been in Kirkmalcolm Brian had taken a liking to exploring the empty house, barged in on Sir John and Blake before they had a chance to get either paper or briefcase.

"They had another try at doping me out of the way last night, only by then I'd hidden the paper up the pub chimney. But, like you said, guessing from the state of my hands where I'd put it, they went along to search the village, taking the briefcase with them so that when they found the papers they would have everything they needed for Brian to pull the rabbit out of the hat. Which of course he did."

"How do you know he did?" Fairfield asked. "You can't be sure they took the briefcase or found your hiding place."

"I know they took the case because when I looked for it in the house, it wasn't there. And when I came back after looking in the shed where I'd hidden it once before, the case was back in the lounge. One of them, Blake most likely, had brought it back while I was outside. And I'm assuming they must have found the papers and used them, because otherwise they wouldn't have returned the case. And to support that, I feel pretty certain Brian broke the code because of the way he later came along and did the same job for me while I was asleep."

At which Fairfield looked up sharply. "You mean it was Brian who wrote all that stuff down for you? You told me *you'd* done it. I was wondering about that—the real code—you know. I was going to ask you. You did pull a fast one after all." He was inclined to be resentful.

"A fast one, maybe. But I didn't tell you *I'd* done it. I simply said it was done, or words to that effect." Maskell ran one finger along the weathered stone edge of the plinth. "Just as Brian, seeing the dishes that needed washing, washed them out of habit—arranging them afterwards in some weird mathematical progression that must have made sense to him—so, seeing a puzzle that needed solving, and having tackled the same puzzle only a short while before, solved it out of habit, probably taking no time at all over it, it being merely a repeat performance for him."

"A bloody mobile computer," Fairfield said, grinned briefly at his own description, then took one hand from his pocket in order to touch the bruised side of his head. "Blake, I reckon. So what did I do to upset him—get in the way?"

"One can't say for certain," Maskell said slowly, his finger still following a long-ago pattern in the stone, "but I would think that Blake, certainly on his own initiative, did actually try to kill you as being the best way of getting you out of the way. I think he must have been promised a very large share of the profits to have got him thinking in terms of murder. Nothing must be allowed to stand in the way . . . Or perhaps he's just made that way." He looked up, blinking a little from the sun. "If you want to do anything about it, it's up to you."

"I function best behind a desk." The other showed large white teeth in a grin. "Not behind a gun. Maybe I'll get my own back on the sod one day. Maybe he'll come asking me for a job—" He squinted sideways to see if his message had been understood.

It had. "Yours is safe," Maskell assured him. "So is your—fee—would you call your promotion? And your bonus."

"Fair enough." Taking his hands from his pockets, Fairfield

stood up, stretching, sweatered arms high above his shaggy black head. He revolved to search the sky. "And what time is our transport due?"

"Not for a while yet." Maskell looked at his watch. "Late lunch for both of us. I timed it to give me time to have this talk with you and then pay a visit."

"A visit?" The other jerked his head in the general direction of the village. "Sir John Whatsit? Foot on his neck and all that sort of stuff? A quiet gloat?"

"Not my style," Maskell told him. "No, I was hoping to persuade you to show me the way to the Pudsey underground menage."

"I knew it," Fairfield said. "The luscious Selena. Midnight and moonlight, black nylon and satin. How's that for sheer poetry?" He grinned. "Although when I met her she was introduced as 'my lass Clara' and she was wearing—Christ, what was she wearing?—some sort of blouse and skirt. What's the attraction, then?"

"Curiosity," Maskell told him, pushing himself away from the weathered stone. "Sheer curiosity."